©

PART 1:
First, Get the Money!

On a silly, sadistic quest for financial freedom, three frenemies search for love in all the wrong places.

Written by:
Torthell J. Robinson

Published By Written By Torthell
A division of Book Collection by T
www.BookCollectionbyTorthell.com

This book is a work of fiction. Characters and events within this book are fictitious, and any resemblance to actual persons, living or dead, is a product of the author's imagination.

Copyright© 2024 by Torthell Robinson

All Rights Reserved

Paperback - 978-1-7377217-3-4

PROLOGUE

Twenty years ago, a competitive Monopoly showdown was underway. Ten-year-old Terrence Ware and eleven-year-old Justice Cole battled it out as the bankrupted eleven-year-old Brandon Perez shuffled a deck of cards on the side.

Terrence, the battleship game piece, parked on the B & O RAILROAD space. He owned all the red and orange properties, each one with a hotel. He also held a majority of the Monopoly money. Justice held the racing car game piece with very little cash to stay in the game. He owned all green and yellow properties and had a few houses on them. It was Justice's turn to roll the dice, this after he had rolled two consecutive doubles that landed him on the FREE PARKING space.

"Roll another double, and you're going to jail, Justice," said Terrence.

Justice grabbed the dice and rolled a three. He hesitated to move his game piece because his next move would land him on Terrence's red property, which had a hotel on it. Terrence grew smug, realizing he'd bankrupted Justice and the game was over. Terrence flashed a shit-eating grin.

An irate Justice swiped all the pieces off the gameboard. "I don't wanna play your stupid game anymore."

"Aww… Justice is sentimotional, again!" Terrence said.

"Sentimotional ain't even a word," said Brandon.

"Ain't ain't a word either," Terrence said.

"What does sentimotional mean, anyway?" a curious Justice asked.

"It's when you're acting sensitive and emotional because you suck at Monopoly."

"I don't wanna play your stupid game anymore," Justice said as he pouted.

"Just say you're mad because you suck."

"I don't suck. You cheated!"

"I'm no cheater. You can't count."

"Yes, I can, Terrence!"

"Okay, bet! Prove it! What's nine times seven?"

Justice utilized his fingers while calculating the equation in his head.

"It's sixty-three," Brandon said.

"Nobody asked you, Brandon!" Justice shouted.

"At least he knew the answer, dummy," Terrence said with a giggle.

"At least my family's not poor like yours." The room grew silent. Justice had said the quiet thing out loud.

Terrence took a moment to calm down but the words were too triggering for him to not lash out. Suddenly, Terrence grabbed the board and smacked Justice upside his head with it. Justice retaliated by tackling Terrence to the ground. The two boys rolled around on the floor.

"Fight! Fight! Fight!" Brandon instigated as he picked up all the Monopoly money off the floor before dashing out of the room.

CHAPTER 1

They say, "Whatever Happens in Vegas Stays in Vegas," but that only applies to money. When you leave this town, you take home the hangovers, the photos capturing your drunken degradation, along with any financial grief or STDs you may have contracted from being an irresponsible slut. But there is a different side to Vegas beyond the strip unknown to those who do not live here. I will tell you a little bit about my side of living in this big, small town.

It was a random Thursday night in the historic heart of Las Vegas's bustling downtown, an area locals frequent to avoid the conundrum of the Las Vegas Strip. The Strip is a tourist trap and a money pit that I avoid. I will only go out to the Vegas Strip or downtown for special occasions such as concerts, sporting events, or when some of my favorite relatives come to visit.

Who wants to be around all that loud music and egotistical unaware drunk idiots, while paying for expensive watered-down drinks? But that night, I had no other choice. It was Ladies' Night at the once-swanky Allure Lounge. There were beautiful women wrapped in sexy gowns sprinkled throughout the lounge, staring at their phones and taking pictures of themselves. Most of them were not interacting with anyone. Despite the decent crowd, the dilapidated bar was not the heavyweight hype it was several years ago.

Two sophisticatedly dressed gents were in a discreet part of the lounge people-watching from a bar off to the side. One of the guys was my childhood best friend Justice Cole, a curly-haired pretty boy, and the burly, good-looking fellow sitting next to him was me, Terrence Ware. We were days away from this fool's wedding date, and he had me out here in these streets.

An intoxicated party guest was in the process of hounding down a strikingly gorgeous lady dressed in a tight, red Cushnie Et Ochs skirt. As the lady attempted to maneuver through the crowded bar area, the inebriated guest beelined right in her direction. He whispered something in her ear and the two of them approached the bar. Moments later, the cavalier handed the lady a drink, leaned in, and attempted to kiss her. She dodged his effort, then threw the cocktail in his face. Security guards swooped in to mediate the situation.

Next to that chaos was a go-go dancer with a very familiar face that I had not seen in over a year. Once I saw her, I could not take my eyes off her. Shontae Hillman. A classic beauty with long, flowing curls and gorgeous caramel skin. Something radiated from within her, rendering her irresistible to everyone. She stood alone as she swayed her hips side to side with the music. She was the apple of my eye but also my first love. I never loved anyone like I loved Shontae. I could not shake her off of me. And this was coming from a guy that has cut off a shit ton of people. I was still in love with her for some reason. There was not a day that went by that I did not think about her. This bothered me to the core. How could my feelings remain the same after a year had passed since our breakup?

"Did you see her?" Justice asked.

I snapped out of my thoughts and nodded yes. "Did you get it?"

Justice dug into his pocket, grabbed his phone, and scanned through his notifications. "Yep! Thank you, sir. Pleasure doing business with you."

"Pleasure doing business with you, my ass! That wasn't business. You had insider information."

"Why, Tee, whatever do you mean?" Justice said with a bit of sarcasm. "Maybe betting against me isn't your game."

"You knew she'd be here because you work with her."

"You shouldn't have bet half of your paycheck that you'd never see her again."

"That was a year ago. I was in my feelings when I made that bet."

"Your fault! A bet is a bet," Justice said. "But I've been on a little hot streak. I won my fantasy football league."

"What was the buy-in?"

"One thousand."

"What?! A thousand dollars, bro?"

"Yep, I won seven grand as first place. Second place got a couple of thousand, and third place broke even," Justice said.

"I wish I could afford to make money swings like that."

"There are opportunities everywhere."

"Like what?"

"Knocking off a church."

"Knock off a church? What kind of heathen do you think I am, Justice?"

"The kind of heathen that goes on ridiculous church rants."

"I do not go on ridiculous church rants. I just don't believe that religion is the gateway to eternity. And while we're broaching the subject, some preachers are like strippers. They play with your emotions, take your money, then leave you questioning yourself."

Justice and I paused as the church rant was acknowledged.

"We're going to hell anyway," Justice said. "Why not make some money and have fun before we go?"

"WE aren't going anywhere because I'm not going to hell."

"I can name at least ten specific moments of things you've done that guarantee you will."

I thought about all the foolish things Justice and I had done over the years while living in Las Vegas and all I could do was nod my head. "Touché."

"See that guy there?" Justice pointed at a heavily tatted man hustling across the club.

"What's so special about him?"

"That's Hollywood. The company I work for wants to buy the club from him. His family's net worth is three billion dollars."

The only billionaires I'd seen were on television. "What would you do if you were a billionaire?"

Justice thought about the question for a second. "I'd buy a yacht with a helicopter pad; I'd have a mansion off all of the coasts. I'd get a Lambo, a Ferrari. What about you?"

"I'd create generational wealth for my family."

"Can you purchase generational wealth from the Gucci store?"

A frown formed on my face as I flashed an irritated gaze at Justice, who shrugged it off.

"Creating generational wealth just sounds boring."

"So, being selfish is fun?"

"Call it whatever you want," Justice said with a shrug as he took a sip from his drink. "I'm about the good life."

"I can't afford the good life right now because I'm stuck in life playing checkers at that stupid ass job. I'm tired of living from paycheck to paycheck, working at a place I hate. I'm ready to play chess with my money. I wanna be free."

"I guess," Justice said.

"What do you mean '*I guess*? You don't want to be free?"

"Free from what, Terrence? It's over for me. I'm getting married in a few days."

"I'm talkin' about financial freedom, bro. Flashy cars and designer clothes don't make you rich. Real wealth is having the freedom to spend your time exactly how you want. That's the ultimate chess move. Don't you wanna be a boss?"

"I'm a senior vice president at my company. I'm kinda a boss," Justice said.

"Yep, and the president of the company can fire you. All I'm saying is I don't wanna wake up forty-something years from now and have to depend on the government to take care of my family. I don't wanna outlive my money."

"That sounds great and all, but I came to the club to get that off my mind. I'm in over my head with debt because of this stupid wedding and that stupid IVF procedure," Justice said with a pout.

"So, you jerked off in a cup?"

"Basically."

"So, when your child asks, where do babies come from, you're going to say—"

"Magazines." Justice downed the last sip of his drink. "I could've hired two sex slaves for the amount of money I spent trying to do the right thing and start a family." Justice took a deep breath. "But I won't complain. I recently closed on a multifamily rental property."

"Nice! Playing Monopoly in real life."

A tense cloud of silence blanketed us as tension brushed across our faces. Hearing or saying the word Monopoly triggers PTSD. Justice and

5

I had played several games of Monopoly during our childhood, and every match we played ended in some traumatic way.

"My apologies for saying that word."

"It's cool," Justice said meekly.

The bartender approached us. She was pretty, beautiful even, but in a fit, toned-down way.

"It's the last call. Can I get you guys anything else?"

"Two shots of Don Julio 1942 for the groom-to-be, who just closed on a rental property. And me. I saved fifteen percent on my auto insurance."

"Make that a double," Justice said.

"A double?" I said as I turned toward Justice. "Do you know how much one shot of Don Julio 1942 is?" This was why I did not like to go out. I was paying for his drinks, and he had way more money than me. But I was involuntarily chosen as the best man for his wedding. "Whatever, make it a double."

She poured two shots. We clinked glasses and downed the shots. I handed the bartender my debit card, and she walked off. Moments later, I noticed a tear rolling down Justice's cheek.

"Justice! What…the…entire…fuck…is wrong with your face? You're being sentimotional in public."

Justice took a few moments to compose himself. "I don't wanna get married anymore."

"I wish you'd said something earlier. I could've stayed my ass home."

"I feel like I've been muscled into the whole marriage thing."

"You are the one that asked that woman to marry you, fool!"

"I think I'm going through a midlife crisis."

"Midlife crisis? You're only thirty, bro."

"I just don't think I'm marriage material," Justice said. "I still sleep with random women. I want to do ignorant things like lines of cocaine off strippers. I need thrills in my life. I'm not domesticated enough for the marriage life." Justice closed his eyes and sighed. "There are things I have accomplished during my life but for the most part, I feel like I've wasted a lot of my life doing things other people wanted me to do. Will *I* ever come first?"

"I get it. I feel like I've wasted my twenties doing things society said I needed to do, never accomplishing anything I wanted. But I also wish I were marrying a woman I loved," I said as I stared across the club at Shontae who was several feet away serving drinks to a bunch of drunk guys in suits.

As Justice reached up to wipe a tear from his eyes, my eyes flickered down at his wrist, where a glimmering timepiece rested. "We've been together for so many years, and people kept saying I should put a ring on it. I think the pressure got to me. Hell, I don't know if I'm even in love with her."

"That's a 'You Problem.' You slept with your best friend's little sister when I advised you not to. You bought a ring when there was no need to. You asked her to marry you when you didn't want to. And you dragged me into this mess by asking me to be your best man when you shouldn't have."

"I'm in over my head. I need to call this whole thing off."

"Name one solid reason why you should call off the wedding?"

"Sex. We have sex once a week. That once-a-week sex will eventually turn into twice-a-month. Turning me into a perverted horny old man. By statistics, we'd end up getting divorced anyway. Why not stop it before the inevitable happens?"

"As the best man, I have to discourage you from calling off the wedding. Even if I didn't mind you calling it off and preventing me from hanging around Brandon more than I wanted to."

"Why do you hate him so much?

"I don't hate him. I think the people who tolerate him daily are the real heroes. He's a con artist that I despise being in my space. He's always running around committing petty crimes and getting away like he's the damn gingerbread man. Have you seen him lately?"

"It was a few months ago. Brandon borrowed a dollar from me to get some gas."

"A dollar for gas? That's walking distance."

Justice reached up to wipe the remaining tears from under his eyes, and he caught my subtle glances at his watch and grinned knowingly. "Oh, I know you see it," Justice's cocky ass said, lifting his hand to give the watch a twirl, making the light dance off its polished surface. "When the lights hit the ice… it twankle and glistens," he said with a chuckle, quoting a Big Tymers song.

I nodded with appreciation. I was in awe of the intricacies, the glistening dial, and the accuracy of its every movement, and I couldn't take my eyes off it. It was an exceptional wristwatch, a monument to elegance and artistry. I couldn't help but feel a twinge of envy and devotion. Although my watch did not match Justice's, we were friends, and he had impeccable taste and flair. "It's… stunning," I said humbly.

"It's a handcrafted, limited-edition masterpiece from Switzerland. It took me forever to find it," said Justice, proud of himself. "I bought myself the watch as a present after closing a major deal last quarter."

The lady in the red dress walked by Justice and stared him up and down as if she wanted to lick him. He took a few moments to reflect. "Love is cursed by monogamy. Why would God create men with all this sperm if he only wanted us to be with one woman?"

The bartender returned. "I'm sorry… your card declined."

I dug into my pocket, pulled out a hundred-dollar bill, and slid it to the bartender. "Oh, I'm sorry. I'm broke again. Between rent and losing that stupid bet you tricked me into, I'm down to my last hundred."

Justice chuckled and stood to his feet. "I'm out. I have to hurry home and not have sex with my fiancée." He leaned in to dap me up. He navigated through the dwindling crowd and exited the club.

The bartender brought back change, which consisted of a ton of $1 bills.

I studied the wad of one-dollar bills. Some were extra flimsy. "What's with all of the dollar bills?"

"We're running low on the big bills tonight," the bartender said.

I examined the bills. "They don't make money like they used to." I tipped the bartender with the loose singles, stood from the bar, and maneuvered through the lounge. I managed to sneak around the lounge and creep up from behind Shontae and shout, "Shontae Hillman!"

"Oh my God! Terrence," she said, startled. She leaned forward and hugged me.

"Wow! You look amazing as always. How have you been?" I asked.

"Good. Life has been good!" Some moments of silence slid between us as we both stared at each other. "It's been a while."

"I tried to call you once after the breakup, but some old Asian lady answered."

"I changed my number."

"I understand. Let's reconnect." I handed Shontae my phone.

"Terrence, there's nothing else to discuss. You broke up with me."

"I only wanted what was best for you. I never wanted to leave you." I took a deep breath and was prepared to lay it all out for her. "Shontae… look… I'm still in lo—"

"This guy!" Victor Michaels, the tall and dapper gentleman, said as he slithered up from behind and placed his arm around my Shontae. "Of all the women in town, and you decide to stalk mine," an irked Victor said.

We stared at each other firmly for a few moments.

"Let's get out of here, babe," Victor said as he rolled his eyes at me. They walked off and headed toward the exit.

"Okay, bet! It's on." At that moment, all I could do was nod. Victor is with the woman I am supposed to spend the rest of my life with, and I was prepared to do whatever it took to get Shontae away from him.

CHAPTER 2

Meanwhile, beneath the Allure Lounge in a private decadent speakeasy was a high-stakes, no-limit, Texas Hold'em poker match. Some of the town's most social elite sat around the fancy traditional cherrywood poker table. Sitting next to the dealer was Reverend Murray Hillman, an opportunistic televangelist and founder of the non-denominational Planet Changers House based in North Las Vegas. Behind his crisp suits and immaculate demeanor was a cunning, stern businessman. Reverend Hillman was known for treating his church not as a place of worship but as a profitable enterprise. Faith to him was a business and business was booming.

To Reverend Hillman's left, puffing on a Fuente Fuente Opus X cigar, was Jorge "Hollywood" Sanchez, the heavily tattooed owner of the Allure Lounge. Hollywood wore his crimes like they were a second skin—literally. His arms were covered in inked serpents, skulls, and dollar signs, each representing a deal or a life he claimed. Hollywood was the kind of guy whose grin was as sharp as the expensive suits he wore.

Next to him was a city councilman and owner of the Houston Commercial Realty Group, Dallas Houston. The middle-aged man's name carried weight around Las Vegas, but not for the reasons most would expect. Mr. Houston's official business was lucrative enough, it was his moonlighting that defined him. His presence was unsettling. Though he dressed like a tech geek, his tiny beady eyes darted around with an intensity that froze the room.

To Mr. Houston's left with a mischievous smirk was Brandon Perez, a scruffy kleptomaniac with sticky fingers and a degenerate gambler in his early thirties. Brandon had a knack for mischief. He was always calculated and scheming for opportunities. Brandon found it hard to resist the thrill of pocketing things that were not his. From the unkempt hair and a permanent five o'clock shadow, Brandon looked like trouble from a mile away. But buried beneath his debauched criminal façade was a faint spark of decency. The minimum buy-in for this poker game was $20,000. The blinds for the poker game were set at $1,000 and $2,000. The dealer button was on Reverend Hillman. Hollywood tossed in the small blind $1,000 burgundy poker chip. Brandon threw in the big blind $2,000 light-blue poker chip.

"It costs you more money keeping the Allure Lounge open than what you make from it," Mr. Houston said. "This place is too prime of a location to be wasted on a traditional club."

"And what would you do differently?" Hollywood asked.

"We—me and you—turn this place into a dispensary that is also a lounge. It would be like Planet 13 but better. Cannabis-infused liquor. We add a smoker's lounge. It would be the ultimate Vegas Experience for smokers across the world."

"Okay. Then, why won't you sell your wife's club?" Hollywood said with a snark.

"I would but it's in a shitty area. Besides, my wife loves that place."

Hollywood took a long pull from his cigar and blew out the smoke. "Speaking of your wife. She sure is a hot piece of ass."

"You know her?" Mr. Houston asked with jealous curiosity.

"Boy, do I! Tell her I said hello," Hollywood said with a cocky chuckle.

Mr. Houston lobbed a menacing glare at Hollywood, then over in Brandon's direction. Brandon sheepishly lowered his head.

"Tonight is a good night… so I'll tell you what. If I win this hand, we'll talk some more. If I lose, don't bring it up the rest of the night."

"Fair enough," Mr. Houston said with a nod that concealed his rage.

The dealer pitched each player two cards. They each studied their hand. The bet was now on Mr. Houston. He threw out a $1,000 chip to call. The bet was now on Reverend Hillman. He studied his hand for a few moments. He tossed in a $1,000 chip to call. Hollywood threw in a burgundy chip to reach the call. The option was now on the stone-faced Brandon, who sat on a pocket pair of aces: Ace of Diamonds and Ace of Spades.

"I'll raise," Brandon said as he tossed in two $2,000 chips.

"Raised to six thousand," the dealer shouted.

Reverend Hillman tossed in his two cards and rose from the table. "That escalated fast."

"I'll meet you at the church later," Mr. Houston mumbled to Reverend Hillman.

Reverend Hillman gave a slight nod, right before he walked away. The dealer picked up his cards and threw them in the muck pile. The bet was now on Mr. Houston. He studied his hand for a few seconds and tossed in four burgundy chips to match the pot.

"Call." The dealer aimed his attention toward Hollywood. "Six thousand dollars is the bet."

Hollywood matched the bet. The dealer gathered the chips to the center. The dealer took the top card from the deck and "burned" it, facedown, under the pot. The dealer placed an Ace of Clubs, a 10 of Clubs, and a 10 of Diamonds face up on the table. The bet was on Hollywood. He tapped the table to check the bet to Brandon, who had on a boat: Aces full of 10s, on the flop. Brandon tossed out a $5,000 brown poker chip.

"Five thousand dollars is the bet."

The action was now on Mr. Houston, who studied his hand. Frustration washed across his face as he cast an irritated gaze at Brandon. Mr. Houston studied his hand again before tossing in his cards.

The dealer grabbed his cards and threw them in the muck pile. "Five thousand dollars is the bet."

Hollywood glanced at his hand a moment and studied Brandon for a few seconds. "What are you sitting on, Chico?" Hollywood grabbed two $5,000 chips and tossed them onto the table. "I'll raise."

"Raised to ten thousand dollars," the dealer uttered. The action was back on Brandon, who grabbed five $1,000 chips and threw them on the table to match the call. The dealer gathered the chips, once again burned a card, and placed a 7 of Clubs face up on the table.

"All in," Hollywood said with a smirk as he pushed all of his chips to the center.

Brandon did not flinch as he threw out another brown chip, signaling a call. Hollywood tossed out a 9 of Clubs and an 8 of Clubs to reveal a flush. Brandon turned over his cards.

"Hijo de puta!" Hollywood shouted as he pounded the table out of frustration.

The dealer pushed the winning pot of $44,000 to Brandon.

A livid Mr. Houston stormed out of the room without saying another word. The door slammed shut behind his exit. Brandon placed a large, hefty trash bag on the table.

"Mind if I exchange these one-dollar bills for bigger bills at the cashier?"

"Again?" Hollywood studied the bag full of loose $1 bills. "Are you some kind of exotic dancer?"

"Uh… yeah!" Brandon said. "And I don't like carrying George Washingtons in my pocket. He owned slaves."

"Whatever. Do as you may. Money is money."

A devilish smirk flashed across Brandon's face. "You're right about that, sir! Money is money!"

CHAPTER 3

Growing up in Las Vegas, you expect to see attractive women everywhere. But I only had eyes for her. Her laughter filled the air as she turned to face me while I took a picture of her with my phone. Her infectious grin illuminated, and her hair hung loosely over her shoulders. She was so perfect to me. Shontae was my forever. There had never been another woman in the world who had made me feel as strongly as Shontae had.

As the sun set, Shontae and I walked hand in hand along the beach, our hearts at ease as we listened to the waves crash against the shore. Shontae paused as she turned to face me, her eyes reflecting the colors of the sunset. "I love you, Terrence," she confessed.

I was overwhelmed with joy. "I love you too, Shontae," I replied.

As we leaned in for a kiss, an unexpected and startling sound interrupted our intimate moment. The constant beeping of the damn alarm clock on my phone jolted me out of my dream.

I smacked the phone to shut it off. I went from a tranquil euphoric feeling of unconditional love to a cold and depressing atmosphere. As I lay with my thoughts, the dream faded away. Since the breakup, I hadn't gone a day without dreaming or thinking about Shontae.

I rubbed my eyes. I felt the crushing weight of my isolation as I looked around my constricted, disorganized bedroom. Shontae cast an eternal shadow over me, serving as a constant reminder of one of the biggest mistakes I had ever made.

I took a deep breath and sighed it all out. I had to face another mundane workday.

I never realized why I was broke until I glanced in the mirror. As I stared at my reflection in the mirror, I saw a cliché: a sucker and a fool that was about to make some stupid corporation richer. I slipped on a red sweater to go over my wrinkled white dress shirt to complete the uniform. If you have not guessed already, I am an insurance agent just like that punk-ass happy-go-lucky Jake from State Farm.

I made my way through the condo and into the living room. I hate waking up early to get ready for a job I hate. Most mornings, I would sit on the couch, imagining there was a million dollars in my bank account. I understand that's not a lot of money, but a million dollars was still a lot for someone who was so broke that their reality check would bounce. I had read books such as *The Secret, Think and Grow Rich, Ask and It Is Given,* and several other books on the laws of attraction and visualization. So far, I had attracted bullshit.

There was jiggling in the door as I heard a key enter the lock. Someone attempted to get into the apartment. I placed my hands together to create a finger gun and took a glimpse through the peephole. It was Emily, Justice's sophisticated cute fiancée.

Emily Perez was pretty in her own right. She had a warm, friendly smile and carried herself with quiet confidence that caught people off guard. Emily's outfit was structured to convey professionalism and comfort. She sported a tailored blouse that was neatly tucked into her ankle-length trousers. The look was completed with a fitted blazer. To the world, Emily appeared as the perfect girl next door. But there was more to her that met the eye. I personally liked her for Justice because she brought a sense of balance to his life. Her calm demeanor grounded him. Compared to the women Justice was attracted to, Emily was more of the responsible choice. Justice was always for women who were 'about that life.' The only life that Emily was about was a life that involved spending the rest of hers with the man of her dreams and starting a family.

"Thanks for opening the door," Emily said. "For some reason, my key didn't work."

"Justice changed the locks yesterday. He's still asleep, I think."

"I'll wake him up," Emily said as she headed for Justice's room.

Justice's condo is a high-rise unit in a complex a few blocks from Fremont Street. The sun peeked through the bedroom window and awakened Justice, who was still in bed.

Emily stared at herself in a mirror as she put the finishing touches of her makeup on her face. Justice walked over and stood behind Emily. His hands made their way down to her waist and slowly slid until they landed under her curvaceous bottom. He started to kiss the back of her neck.

A giggling Emily pushed Justice off of her. "Stop, babe. I'm running late. I forgot that my makeup was over here."

"Terrence left for work already. You can be as loud as you want," said Justice.

"No. He's still here, and I have to get to work. Besides, had you not stayed out so late and stopped by when I asked you to, you could've had a piece last night."

"You sure do know how to ruin morning-wood. I missed those freaky quickie girlfriend days."

"I do too, but work has been so stressful. I promise, after the wedding, it all will be worth it," Emily said as she kissed Justice on the forehead. "I can't wait to spend the rest of my life in love with you, Justice."

But Emily's statement did not excite Justice as he took a hard beat to reflect. "Emily, about the wedding, I..."

"Oh, I meant to ask, have you and Terrence talked yet?"

"Not quite but—"

"The lease is up at my place, and I don't want to move into some bachelor pad. I know you guys have been roommates since high school, but don't you think it's time you boys become men and establish your independence from each other?"

"Yeah, but—"

"What happens after we get married?" Emily said as she started to pace around the room in search of something.

"I haven't gotten to that part yet," Justice said. "I have a lot of other things to deal with before conversing with Terrence about our living situation. But I'll talk with him."

"Have you seen a thumb drive laying around anywhere? It has my client's financial records on it."

"No, but I'll keep an eye out for it."

Justice grabbed Emily, and they started to make out. Soon, Emily finally pushed him off her.

"Baby, stop. Not right now. I have to go. Please have fun with your boys this weekend." Emily kissed Justice on the lips one final time. "See you on our wedding day." Emily gathered herself and exited the room.

Justice's phone rings. "This is Justice...Yes, sir...I'll be there shortly."

Justice jumped to his feet and rushed to the bathroom.

Several moments later, Emily re-entered the living room.

"Bye, Terrence," Emily said as she walked through the condo. "Don't party too hard this weekend."

Bitch, I am broke, I thought but instead said, "I most certainly will try not to."

Emily exited the condo as Justice entered the living room.

"I need you to help me move some things," Justice said. "It will be quick, and it's in the same area as your job."

"Ok. What do you need to move?"

"Some of Emily's stuff. I need to move into her new apartment."

"New apartment? Is that why you changed the locks on the door?"

A standoffish Justice folded his arms. "I had to. Her lease was up and she wanted us to live together," an annoyed Justice said.

"I could be wrong, but isn't that protocol for engaged couples?"

"I guess. If we even get there," Justice said as he shrugged his shoulders. "I just don't want Emily to have access to my place anymore. So, are you helping me move her things out or not?"

"Man, hell no! You must think I'm a new fool. I will not have blood on my hands. You're on your own," I said and walked out of the condo leaving Justice alone with his thoughts.

CHAPTER 4

Las Vegas is a city built on illusions, where riches can be gained and lost with a card flip. For Brandon, a Las Vegas local with more ambition than common sense, the city's gloss provided the ideal backdrop for his next scheme: blanketing the whole metro area with counterfeit one-dollar bills. Brandon had created a stockpile of counterfeit one-dollar bills and put his plan into action.

Brandon sat at a wooden table in a dimly lit cheap motel room in downtown Las Vegas, a few blocks from Fremont Street. He was surrounded by cigarette smoke-stained walls and an aged bulb that threw spooky shadows. If these walls could talk, what disgusting things would they reveal? The walls were thin as car engines, honking horns, and laughter contrasted with Brandon's precise craftsmanship inside.

A coin-shaped printer, ink bottles, precision tools, and cash-like paper stacks sat on the tabletop. The chair creaked as he shifted over to examine the numerous stacks of false money. There was an enormous stack of counterfeit one-dollar bills. Brandon spent several weeks in this dirty motel room, under a flickering desk lamp, replicating the fine features of authentic one-dollar bills. There were many stacks of vacuum-sealed one-dollar bills, a tan bag, and two duffle bags.

Brandon began to fill the duffel bags with counterfeit dollars. One was allocated for the sealed bills, while another was a loose single with the instruments he needed to print his bills. He gathered the remainder of his belongings and exited the cheap hotel.

His first destination was a prominent downtown cafe named Parlour, a brunch eatery with a unique twist on classic dishes in a contemporary environment. He walked in, ordered crème brûlée French toast, and when the bill arrived, he nonchalantly slipped the waitress a stack of fake one-dollar bills.

Brandon spent the remainder of the morning bouncing from one establishment to another. He popped into souvenir shops, convenience stores, and even a weird pawn shop owned by a blind elderly guy named Gus. The phony bills went undetected wherever he went. It felt almost too easy.

His next visit was to Freemont Street. Brandon understood he had to be more cautious here since the casinos were known for their cutting-edge security. He opted to start small with a casino that appealed more to locals than high-rolling visitors.

Walking into the Golden Nugget, Brandon felt a surge of exhilaration. The air was heavy with thick cigarette smoke and the continuous clinking of gambling machines. He proceeded to the bar, got a drink, and paid with another stack of fake bills. The bartender, a big man with a four-leaf clover tattoo on his forearm, did not attempt to examine the bills, making Brandon's heart accelerate. Brandon could hardly control his joy. He took his drink and, feeling invincible, walked up to the blackjack table.

Brandon had effortlessly distributed about twenty thousand dollars in fake bills. However, his luck was soon to run out.

At Circa, Brandon decided to boost the ante. He walked around the magnificent casino, taking in the sights and noises. The gleaming chandeliers and marble flooring made him feel like royalty. He approached the cashier's cage, prepared to exchange a hefty wad of twenty counterfeits for chips.

The cashier, a sharp-eyed lady with a no-nonsense approach, skimmed over the money and scowled. Brandon's heart sank as she picked up the phone and spoke into it. Within minutes, two hefty security officers came to Brandon's side.

"Sir, we need to speak with you," one of them said, his tone leaving no space for dispute.

Brandon attempted to keep things calm. "Is there a problem?"

The guard did not bother to respond. He just took Brandon by the arm and led him to a tiny, windowless room in the back of the casino. Brandon's mind raced, attempting to think of an exit strategy.

The chief of casino security, a stern man with a high and tight military hairstyle, entered the room and sat down across from Brandon. He laid down the counterfeit bills on the table one by one.

"Can you explain these?" he questioned, his tone chilly.

Brandon gulped hard. "Uh, I must have gotten them from a... shady strip club."

"What club is that?"

"I'm guessing the Velvet Room off of Spring Mountain," said Brandon.

Unexpected commotion outside the door stopped Brandon from digging himself any deeper. The security head scowled and proceeded to investigate, leaving Brandon alone for a few moments. Brandon seized the chance, examining the room and noticing an air vent near the ceiling.

Brandon rushed atop the table and tugged the vent cover off in a fit of urgency and agility he hadn't realized he possessed.

He wiggled into the tight conduit, disregarding his claustrophobia, which threatened to overpower him. He had no clue where he was heading, but anything was preferable to confronting the wrath of the casino security staff. After what seemed like an eternity of crawling, he discovered another vent cover and kicked it open, emerging into a janitor's closet.

Brandon brushed himself off from the dust and gently opened the closet door. He looked both ways and noticed the coast was clear. He slipped out and dashed to the nearest exit. Brandon disappeared among a crowd of visitors as he exited the casino.

Brandon took a long breath, allowing the desert air to fill his lungs. He realized he'd pushed his luck too far this time. There were other ways of converting these bills into real cash. As he walked away from the Strip's casinos' bright lights and wild energy, Brandon couldn't help but giggle at the ridiculousness of the situation. He may have been a small-time criminal, but he had a plan he intended to execute. And in Las Vegas, that was more valuable than all the money in this town, real or counterfeit.

CHAPTER 5

America! Home of the free... I think. Well, at least, that is how it is marketed. I do not feel free, especially after a visit to the bank. Some say money does not buy happiness, but creeping up on thirty years of life, I've come to realize that only broke people say that.

I approached an intersection where the light was red. A few moments had passed and the light turned green. The car in front of me did not budge as cars in the lanes next to us started to move forward. I politely laid into my horn and sped pass the car to get a better glance at the person driving. Some idiot staring at his phone. One of the biggest epidemics on the planet was the creation of smartphones. They have dummified humanity. Have you seen the crop of humans that are outside these days? They are the ones clogging up the aisleways at your local grocery store and causing all the car accidents on the damn streets.

I usually park my car under a parking garage a few blocks from my workplace. I do not want to put that many miles on my car, and it costs a fortune to keep gas in it. Did you know Americans owe more than

$1.2 trillion in auto loans? And guess what? I was one of those fools stuck with one of them. The borrower is a slave to the lender. The car I own—correction, the car the bank allowed me to think that I own—is relatively new. It was all good until I started making payments on the damn thing. I knew it would be a liability whenever I financed it, but I wanted to maintain my flyness. It was exciting when I test-drove it and even more ecstatic when I drove it off the lot, not realizing the car had depreciated several thousand dollars. The vehicle's value continues to decline as years and miles accumulate. And please do not get me started on the overpriced monthly car insurance bill I pay.

However, I have realized that most of the debt that I had accumulated was established because I wanted to impress some random person who probably did not give a damn about me in real time. Maintaining an image is the real American Dream and where most American dollars are wasted. And why should anyone want to impress these fools in our society?

There was a small line of people waiting to see the bank teller as I moseyed up to the nearby ATM to check my bank account balance. My phone rang, and I noticed an incoming call from Mom. Suddenly, an older gentleman with a walker popped out of nowhere and deliberately cut in front of me.

"Excuse me, sir," I said sternly but kind. "Sir, the line starts behind me."

The grumpy, old man hurled an ugly glare at me. He disrespectfully continued to move up front. I decided to regain my place and re-cut back in front of him.

"Sum-bitch."

"What was that?" I said as I turned my attention to the old man. I noticed that he was flipping me off.

"I called you a sum-bitch," the old man said, reaffirming what I thought he'd said.

"I really don't have the time or the crayons to explain this to you, but did you mean son-of-a-bitch, you illiterate dotard?"

"No. I meant fuck you and your mother, you motherfucker."

I felt my fist ball up. Nobody talked about my mother to my face, so I stepped to the old man. I stared him cold dead in his face for a few seconds. We stared each other down like an old Western showdown. "I'll eat the meat off of your bones and hang your skeleton in my closet next to the last person that said something about my mother."

"You're not a good neighbor like the commercial says," the terrified old man said, as he reached up and turned his hearing aid down. I proceeded to the ATM and conducted my transaction. The ATM produced a receipt. The receipt showed a balance of a negative seven dollars and thirty-nine cents. In a fiery fury, I commenced to kicking the shit out of that stupid, yet innocent, cash machine.

"Should've let me go first, you broke, sum bitch," said the taunting old man as he began to make it rain on me as if he were tipping a stripper.

The root of all evil is not money. It's the lack of money that is the root of all evil. People rob, kill, or go ballistic on ATMs for lack of money. A police officer approached the ATM. I calmed myself down and continued on with my journey to my dead-end job, which was in the building next to this stupid bank.

It sure is hard to go to work when you are broke, especially after getting paid the day before. I entered the insurance agency office and headed for the elevator.

"Hold the elevator," said Victor Michaels, my casually dressed cocky nemesis, who was approaching from a distance.

I looked around frantically, searching for something to grab. "I don't have anything to hold on to."

Victor flung an angry expression at me as the elevator doors closed.

As the elevator went up, I reflected on how working with Victor was a constant reminder of the once-in-a-lifetime love I had fumbled. When Shontae and I were together, she said Victor was just a friend, but he was just lingering around waiting for the perfect moment to pounce. The breakup with Shontae happened several months earlier. Not only was it difficult to let go of our three-year romance, but now our time together haunts me because the guy she is dating is a coworker.

Victor had been Shontae's best friend for over ten years, she explained. They met back in college. She always discussed their connection, especially while she and I were dating. Her father had always preferred Victor over me, arguing that because he had graduated from college, he was more polished, stable, and reliable than me.

Shontae always tried to convince me that her relationship with Victor was harmless, strictly platonic, and that there was never any romantic history between them. "Victor is just a friend," I remembered Shontae saying. But I knew better. I would always tell her, "He appears to see you as more than just a friend." Even though I sensed there was more, she dismissed it as paranoia and jealousy.

However, when Shontae and I split, everything changed. I found out that one day Victor had come over to her house to comfort her after our breakup. He consoled her, showed her that he understood how she felt. His arms soothed her as they cuddled up on the couch and watched a movie. Something changed about halfway through the film. Their first kiss rapidly grew into a passionate night of lovemaking and that fool finally weaseled his way in. But if you have been in the game long enough, you have either been the friend or the victim of the infamous *friendzone*.

Victor had patiently waited like a vulture for the right moment, playing the long game, and, ultimately, he took over a part of Shontae's life from where I was supposed to be. That was a difficult pill to swallow. I needed to figure out how to move on, regardless of the agony.

The elevator doors opened, and I walked over to my workspace. There was nothing nostalgic about returning to my cubicle. This is my job, the ultimate mundane. Did you know that the word *job* stands for Just-Over-Broke? A job is where workers work hard enough to get fired, and employers pay enough so that employees do not quit. Efficient workers are rewarded with only more work.

What do you call someone who is broke, works a nine-to-five, and has no ambitions? That, my friend, is what society calls the middle class, known to over sixty-six percent of Americans as a reality and understood by me as a horror story titled "Modern-Day Slavery," or, for the use of better terms, "Capitalism." Most of the things you think you own belong to a bank. You're just leasing it. And sure, even if you pay off your house, somebody else will eventually live in it.

My phone rang again, and this time, I answered. "Hey Mama."

"Terrence, do you have some cash I can borrow?"

"Not really… How much do you need?"

"I think close to three thousand dollars."

"I'm sorry, Mom. I don't have it."

"I'm sorry I asked. You already do a lot for us… helping us pay the mortgage and all. Your father said we need it by Monday morning or else…"

"Or else?! What does that even mean? Where's Dad?"

"In jail."

"Jail? What's he in jail for?"

"Tax evasion. I'm married to a con artist, son. He said he was going away for business, but he's been in jail for the past week. He said he needs you to come visit him, and he will explain more."

"Okay. I gotta get back to work."

"Okay, love you."

"Love you, too, Mom." I ended the call, then pulled out a "to-do" list painted with my angry thoughts and other tasks such as: "quit this stupid-ass job," "tell my boss to suck my balls," "burn this bitch down," "put down payment on engagement ring." I added, "Take care of my mother."

Denice, a dorky but spicy hot coworker, walked through the aisle with what appeared to be belongings from her desk. "Bye, guys." Denice continued to mope her way out.

Another coworker dressed in a suit and tie, Ben, approached me from the back. "I hate to see her go but love watching her walk away. Man! Plastic surgeons don't make asses like that. The type of ass you want to bite into."

Guys at every cubicle Denice walked by took a glance at her bottom. She was built like a Goddess. Denise had the kind of physique that had a gravitational pull on men, like the Medusa effect. You could not look away once you stared at her.

"What happened to her?" I asked.

"Cutbacks," said Ben. "The boss man wants to see you."

"For what?"

Ben shrugged, then walked off. I stood, and headed off to the boss's office, and knocked on the door.

"Come in," John shouted. John, the middle-aged, twenty-plus-year manager of the firm finished typing up an email. "Have a seat."

I took a seat.

"Water?"

"Sure."

John placed a bottle of water at the edge of his desk. "So, when I hired you, I explained how positions were subject to change depending on one's work performance. As you already know, our company's going through a lot of changes and downsizing. With that said, I have some good news and some bad news."

"I'd like to hear the good news first."

"Your position is no longer needed and—"

"Wait, that's the good news? You're firing me?" I abruptly asked.

"I think there's a misunderstanding—"

I knocked the bottle of water off the table. "I think it ain't safe for you in this zoo. So yeah, there's about to be a misunderstanding."

"Terrence—"

"I'll burn your house down."

"Terrence—"

"Help you rebuild it and burn that bitch back down to the ground again."

"Terrence, listen—"

"No, you listen. You can't fire me." I proceeded to knock the rest of John's belongings off his desk. "Because I quit! Suck my balls," I said as I stormed off.

Before completely exiting, John said, "The bad news is, I have cancer and you were taking my position."

My reaction to the news froze me at the door. Why did he not lead off with that information before I made an ass of myself? Now I have to commit all the way as the news caught me off guard. I gathered what was left of my ego and exited out of John's office. I poked my chest out and walked as confidently as possible back to my cubicle. Everyone around the office heard the interaction. "A job only pays you enough to be broke," I said out loud as I gathered my possessions. Even though I knew my job was a short-term solution for a long-term problem, I was not quite ready to quit today. But it was what it was. *This will be the last job I ever work again.* I exited the office.

CHAPTER 6

The desert morning sun twinkled on the polished brand-new Chevy Corvette as Justice navigated the busy downtown streets of Las Vegas. The car was a symbol of Justice's hard work and should have brought some semblance of gratification, but it was just another hollow indulgence.

Justice's thoughts floated to Emily and the upcoming wedding. Was he ready to spend the rest of his life with one woman? Justice had a great example of a relationship growing up as he was raised by both of his parents who were still in love with each other after 40 years of marriage. But Justice thought that was a boring way to waste your sex drive.

Justice approached an intersection, and a familiar face caught his attention. At the pedestrian crossway was the gorgeous lady he had locked eyes with the night before. As opposed to the red dress that had garnered several gazes, today, she was in a business casual outfit, her hair was neatly pulled back. The change intensified her attraction, adding sophistication to her sex appeal. Something about her felt like a breath of fresh air more so than the life he had with Emily.

Justice's heart started to race as she walked confidently across the crossway. He swerved the Corvette to the curb and scanned the land for an open parking space.

He passed several parking lots that were full as the desperation mounted each second that she moved away from him. Justice spotted an open spot and pulled into it, barely avoiding a collision with a passing car.

Justice hopped out of the car and chased after her, weaving through the crowd, his mind racing as the sensible part of his brain screamed at him to stop and turn around. He was getting married soon and had a baby on the way. But he had to see her again. The pretty boy playboy needed to see if he still had it.

He finally caught up to her just as she reached the entrance of a Pilates gym in a sleek office building.

"Hey, excuse me," he said breathlessly.

She turned and a mixture of surprise and delight flashed across her face as she recognized Justice. "Yes." She was even more strikingly beautiful up close.

A disarming smile flashed across Justice's face. "I couldn't let you walk past me again. We saw each other last night at the Allure Lounge."

"Yes, I remember you," she said with a smile.

Justice extended his hand. "I'm Justice."

She met his greeting. "I'm Karla. Nice to meet you."

"I couldn't stop thinking about our interaction last night," Justice said.

Karla smiled as her head slightly tilted and her eyes narrowed. "I will save you the trouble. I'm not really in the mood for this kind of conversation. I'm already late for a Pilates class."

"I totally get it. Can we maybe grab coffee someday? No pressure."

There was something in Justice's eye that intrigued her. They were both drawn to each other and not just by a physical attraction. There was a deeper unspoken chemistry that they shared and wanted to explore.

After a few moments of hesitation, Karla sighed. She reached into her bag and pulled out a business card. "Sure, we'll do coffee."

Justice grinned as she handed him the card. "I'll see you soon, gorgeous. Enjoy your class," he said with a wink as he walked away and disappeared into the crowd.

As he walked along the sidewalk, the reality had crept back in. He was days away from marrying Emily. Justice examined the card in his hand. He could not shake the feelings he had with Karla. When he got back into the car, he sat for a while cogitating on his life. And he began to cry like a little boy.

CHAPTER 7

The Arts District of Las Vegas is a vibrant hub full of indie art galleries, and old warehouses converted into theater stages. Amongst the restaurants, shops, and bars is a three-story office building straddling West Charleston Street.

Emily was in her office typing furiously on a desktop computer. On her desk was a picture of her and Justice. Across from her was an antsy Hollywood who paced back and forth. Emily was a CPA for the Bueller & Co. accounting firm that provided business professionals with tax, accounting, and consulting services.

"The lounge made over ninety thousand dollars last night, but the expenses ate up half of the revenue," Emily said as she scanned numbers from her desktop. "What is this forty-four-thousand-dollar expense?"

"Oh…it's nothing," a fidgety Hollywood said, dismissing the charge.

"The Allure Lounge has now become a liability, and you should consider closing it down. That'll save you half a million dollars a month in your overall portfolio.

"You're gorgeous," a deflecting Hollywood said. "Ever gotten knocked up?"

"Uh…thank you," she said confused. "I'm currently engaged, and I am knocked up as we speak."

"I knew it! Congratulations! The pretty ones always get their clubs shot up."

Emily's eyes floated down at the tattoos on Hollywood's hands. "Can we refocus on the reason why you hired us?"

"Sure. Yes. Sell the Allure Lounge. Everyone says I should, but I'm just not doing it. OK. Suggest something different. The Allure Lounge is my baby. What other options do I have?"

"There aren't many options, Mr. Sanchez. You'll have to close the doors of the lounge or stomach another year of declining sales."

"I'm thirsty. You thirsty?"

"No, but there's a vending machine right outside the door."

Hollywood exited the office and walked up to the vending machine. He dug in his pocket and grabbed a wad of cash. He flipped through several $100 bills until he reached a $1 bill. He inserted one of the bills into the vending machine, but the machine rejected it. He placed the dollar back into the machine, but it spit the bill out again. He pulled out another dollar bill and attempted once more. The vending machine spat out this bill too. He tried with a third dollar bill but got the same result.

Hollywood poked his head in Emily's office. "Your machine is broken."

Emily pulled out a couple of $1 bills from her wallet and walked to the vending machine. She stuck a dollar in the machine, and it accepted her bill. "Maybe the machine doesn't like your money," Emily said as she walked back to her office.

Hollywood studied the $1 bills in his stash.

"Mr. Sanchez," a lady said from a distance dressed in a fitted navy suit that accentuated her athletic frame. Her tight ponytail kept her hair out of her face. "We'd like a word with you." The lady exuded an air of composed authority as she moved with calm precision.

Hollywood stared at Emily.

She shrugged her shoulders.

"Who is we?"

The lady flashed her Federal Bureau of Investigation badge. "Special Agent Leslie Thurman," she said firmly, her voice steady as she delivered the Miranda rights to Hollywood. "You have the right to remain silent. Anything you say can and will be used against you in a court of law. You have a right to an attorney. If you cannot afford one, one will be appointed to you. Do you understand these rights as they have been read to you?"

Federal agents surrounded Hollywood and placed handcuffs on him.

"This is bullshit! I didn't do anything," Hollywood pleaded. "I want my lawyer, now!"

Despite the tension of the moment, Agent Thurman's professional confidence showed she was in complete control as the federal agents escorted Hollywood out of the building.

CHAPTER 8

On the other side of town, Justice was seated at his desk. Justice worked as a broker for the Houston Commercial Realty Group, which was a full-service firm specializing in brokerage, property management, commercial real estate, capital markets, and receivership services.

Justice, raised in an affluent Green Valley Ranch neighborhood, was groomed for success from an early age. With every opportunity provided by his parents, in both athletics and academics, he flourished. Leading his class at Stanford University, Justice had landed a highly sought-after job with one of the biggest companies in Las Vegas, the Houston Commercial Realty Group.

On Justice's desk was a beautifully hand-carved wooden chess set and a picture of him with Emily. There was a stack of assignments, pending deals, and an invoice for the upcoming wedding on Justice's desk, too. Justice studied the invoice and shook his head in disbelief at the outrageous $100,000 wedding cost. The office phone rang. An unknown, unrecognized number flashed across the caller ID. Simultaneously, there was a knock at the door.

"Come in," said Justice.

Justice's assistant entered the office and placed a large, sealed envelope on Justice's desk.

"Thanks, Brian." Justice proceeded to answer the call. "This is Justice."

The unrecognized caller blurted out, "What's up, bitch?"

At that moment, Mr. Houston pushed his snarky, smug face through the door.

"One second," Justice said before covering the phone.

Mr. Houston scowled Brian down until the assistant timidly exited the office.

"Everything okay, sir?"

A turtleneck wearing Mr. Houston entered the office and locked the door behind him. "Justice, life sucks. My wife is a slut, and my daughters think I'm an asshole."

The fake smile on Justice's face weakened as he shifted in his seat from the uncomfortable awkward aura that Mr. Houston's statement left in the room. "Uh…um. I'm sorry you feel that way. Is there something I can do for you?"

"No. You've done a lot for me already. I wanted to commend you on the stellar job you've been doing at the firm."

"Thank you, sir! That means a lot coming from you."

"It's looking promising for you. You're at the top of my list for the president position," said Mr. Houston. "We'll talk specifics later." Mr. Houston signaled for Justice to end the call.

Justice placed the phone down.

Mr. Houston leaned in and whispered, "I need a favor from you when you have a moment. No rush but ASAP."

"Sure! What do you need?"

"Are you familiar with the Allure Lounge?"

"I am."

"I need it to disappear."

Justice, confused with the proposal, started to laugh. "Like magic, huh," Justice said, snapping his fingers.

Mr. Houston did not find the request humorous.

Justice regained his professional bearing. "How would I make the Allure Lounge disappear?"

"I'm joking," Mr. Houston said, giving Justice a forced, weird thumbs-up. He patted his pockets. "I have something for you. I'll be right back," he said as he exited.

The office phone rang again. "This is Justice."

"Why did you hang up on me?" the caller asked.

"My apologies. Who is this again?"

"It's Brandon. Where are you?"

"I'm at work like most responsible adults. What the hell are you up to?"

"I'm about to hop into something." From Brandon's perspective, he inched close to an unsecured brand-new black Mercedes-Benz parked on the street, its passenger-side window rolled halfway down. Brandon surveyed his surroundings, then inched closer to the luxury vehicle. His eyes lit up like a Christmas tree as Brandon spotted a Louis Vuitton purse on the passenger seat. "Just a heads up, I booked a suite on the strip. We're staying at the Venetian to kick off the bachelor party."

"Yeah…about the wedding. I need to talk with you about that—"

"Don't worry about the expenses," said Brandon. "I'm taking care of all that."

"No! I can't let you do that, Brandon."

"You're marrying my sister. It'll be my absolute honor and privilege. But this weekend, you're out with the boys. I want us to have a good time. So, I'm granting you something sort of like a hall pass. Let's call it a homeboy pass."

"I'm following," said Justice. "What might this homeboy pass be, pray tell?"

"I'll turn a blind eye during our bachelor party weekend escapades if you promise not to tell my sister and also promise not to do it while you're married."

"Okay, bet! We'll see how things play out," Justice said with a chuckle.

"I'm in the last days of my bachelor life," Brandon declared.

"What? Say it ain't so?"

"Yeah, man! I bought a ring. Let's just hope she says yes," Brandon said as he leaned in the window and grabbed the purse from the seat. But he got stuck in the process. "Send me your address. I gotta go, bro." The phone call ended.

Meanwhile, Justice received another call on the office line. He screened the call, and then decided to answer. "Victor, how's it going, man?"

"All is well, my man. Thanks for your patience with the whole house hunt. I got that promotion at work. We're celebrating at the new place in a couple of days. It is sort of a housewarming party. My girl has some of her friends coming through. And they're kind of hot. You and your boys should pull up."

"Cool. Send me the address and we'll be there."

Mr. Houston shoved his snarky, smug face through the door again. Justice shielded the phone.

"Yes, sir."

Mr. Houston entered the office, walked toward Justice's desk and placed a thumb drive on Justice's desk. "Thank you. I went ahead and promoted you to president of sales because of this," Mr. Houston said, tapping on the thumb drive.

"Victor, gotta go. See you in a few. Okay, bye." Justice ended the call and placed the phone down.

"We'll talk more specifics later," Mr. Houston suggests. "Right now, I need you to fire Shontae. She was the other candidate, but this was her second day coming in late this year."

"But, sir…I just hired her."

"Well, it should be easier to fire her. Especially, since you will have to fire the acting president of the company," Mr. Houston said. His erratic movements throughout the office made Justice feel uneasy.

"I'm not sure I'm comfortable with that," Justice said.

"Sure, you are. I have full confidence in you, it's business, the only place that justifies being an asshole. It's so much fun!" Mr. Houston said with a wink. He gave Justice another psychotic, weird thumbs-up and exited. Moments later, there was another knock at the door.

"Come in."

Shontae entered the office. "Hey, Justice."

Justice is caught by surprise. "Shontae. Hey! It's been a while, huh?"

"Um, not really. I saw you an hour ago."

There's a slight pause between them.

"Oh! Right! But that was a long hour ago. But…uh…how can I help you?"

"I've been meaning to thank you for hiring me," Shontae said. "The nightclub industry was killing me."

"Please, don't mention it," Justice said with a fake smile.

"So, what's up? Mr. Houston said you wanted to see me."

"Uh…yeah, about that."

CHAPTER 9

It was one of those days as I walked through an alley. Remember earlier when I spoke about Capitalism? Let me give you a little more insight into that topic. The school systems in America suck balls because they do not teach financial literacy, which is supposed to be conducted at home by the parents, but who in the hell taught them? Most American parents have gone through the same school system that did not teach financial literacy either. Schools do not teach students how to balance a damn bank account, nor do they teach students about the credit system. The public school system in America does not care to teach students about finances and creating generational wealth because that would impede the process of creating employees.

I grew up a little different than Justice and Brandon. Justice came from a family of entrepreneurs. His family was the Jones on our block everybody tried to keep up with. They come from a long line of robber barons. His father was into real estate and owned a construction company where my father worked. In a way, Justice always acted as if he were better than me because of that. Justice's mother owned a couple of dry cleaners. We spent the majority of our days over at Justice's house because he had all of the cool toys my folks could not afford.

Even though Justice's family appeared rich, Brandon was the closeted rich kid growing up. His grandfather died in a plane crash when he was a baby and left his father a shit ton of money. But Brandon's father put the inheritance as a trust fund for him and his father joined the military to become a fighter jet pilot for the United States Air Force.

Growing up, we never met his mother, who kind of abandoned him. She divorced Brandon's father, Mr. Perez, and re-married some wealthy guy who had two daughters from a previous marriage. The couple lived happily ever after on the other side of town.

Brandon lived in our neighborhood with his father and Emily until middle school. He moved in with his mother across town into a big-ass house in McDonald Ranch of Henderson, Nevada.

Brandon received his trust fund when he turned 21 and quickly gambled most of it away between poker, sports betting, and get-rich-quick schemes.

My upbringing consisted of God-fearing parents who went to church every Sunday. My family was the poor family on the block. We grew up poor, but we did not know. We had a roof over our heads, we had clothes on our backs, shoes on our feet, and food to eat. There were things I wanted growing up that I did not get, but we had everything we needed.

If hard work made you rich, then my parents should have been billionaires. My father was in construction, and my mother was a schoolteacher. They got up every day, went to work, and paid their bills. Their whole lives revolved around the fear of not paying bills. During my childhood, our lives orbited around fear. There was fear the lights would go out from lack of money, fear of getting low grades in school, and fear of making my parents angry. I feared asking my parents for anything and hearing them say, 'We can't afford it,' which felt like the most dismissive words one could have ever uttered.

I would ask, "Why?"

The answer would always be, "I'm broke."

I hated hearing that because the answer killed the idea. I wanted my parents to try harder instead of dismissing it due to the lack of money. The fear of losing could not be greater than the excitement of winning. That was the mindset I wish they had. My dad thought the quickest way to get rich was to write a book about getting rich.

My parents wanted the American dream for my five siblings and me. My parents were popping out kids like the planet was running out of black people. I do not know why these fools decided to have so many kids. My parents believed going to college, receiving a degree, and getting a good job was the only way to make an honest living. But now, the jobs they wanted for us are being outsourced by artificial intelligence.

Economically, I hated how my parents raised me. My folks did not learn much about economics and finances, so we found out the hard way. Hence, one of the reasons why I found myself walking into a payday advance loan center. I proceeded to the next available window.

"How may I help you?" said Monica the receptionist.

"I need to take out a loan of three thousand dollars."

Monica grabbed a form and slid it to me. "Just fill in your name and your social security number, and we'll see what we can do for you."

I jotted down my info on the application and slid it over to her. She started to giggle.

"What's so funny?"

"My boyfriend claimed he thought a coworker named Terrence threw spoiled milk and condoms on his car a few days ago. But I knew it had to be another woman. What guy would do something like that?"

Me, I thought. Yeah, I did that shit. But my curiosity grew. Did she just say what I thought she said? "Victor? You and Victor Michaels date?"

"Yep. We've been dating for the last six years."

"Really?"

"Oh my."

"What's wrong?" I asked curiously.

"Your application declined. To use our services, you need to have at least a 550 score and yours shows it's a 99."

"Ninety-nine what?"

"Your credit score is 99."

There was an awkward beat between us. I gracefully turned around and walked out of the building.

I could not even get a payday loan. But there was still hope for me. A bum on the street gets a dollar every now and again. Which meant anybody could make a dollar.

Suddenly, I stepped into something squishy. It appeared to be dog poop. But a few feet away, I noticed a sleeping homeless man sprawled across the sidewalk with his pants pulled halfway past his ass. A sign was propped up on him that read: *No lies here. I'm in it for booze and weed. Come share your dollar with me.*

I took off the disgraced shoe and placed it next to the homeless man who suddenly awakened and asked, "Got any spare change?"

"If you can ask for a dollar… you can ask for a job application that could lead to more gratifying questions like, 'Would you like ketchup with that order?'"

"You miss a hundred percent of the shots you don't take," the homeless man said, as he rolled over and fell back asleep.

There was wisdom in what the homeless man said as I studied him for a few moments. But one thing I will never understand is where homeless people get pens to write their signs. And I will also never understand how we can live in America amongst some of the world's wealthiest people and have a growing homeless population. Some areas around America look as if they are third-world countries. This country has generated trillions of American dollars to fight pointless wars but cannot do the same for people living here. There are more than 5,000 homeless people in Las Vegas on any given night, and more than 13,000 people will experience homelessness at some point this year. There are close to 600,000 people experiencing homelessness in America.

Many people experience homelessness due to a lack of affordable housing, unemployment, poverty, mental illness, and substance abuse. And some of the people who are homeless can also go home. I do not know what brought this man to these extreme living conditions, but I could help a little. "You want something to eat?"

The homeless man smiled broadly, displaying missing teeth. "Can I have a sandwich?"

"Yes, but first, pull your pants up. You've got all of your business out in the streets."

The bum tucked his shirt in, pulled his pants up, and we carried on our merry little way into a nearby coffee shop.

An eager barista waited to assist customers from behind the cash register. I grabbed a sandwich off the rack and moved over to the register.

"What can I get started for you?"

"I'll take a passion fruit tea and this sandwich."

The bum leaned over and mumbled. "Can you also get me a…"

I covered my nose and leaned away from the putrid murmur. "Don't whisper!"

The bum covered his mouth and said, "Can you get me a large skinny caffè mocha?"

"You're only getting this damn sandwich you asked for!"

"Will the sandwich and tea be it?" asked the barista.

I reached for my wallet, pulled out my last twenty-dollar bill, and handed it to the clerk. She rang me up and gave me back the change. I passed the bum the sandwich, grabbed my drink, and headed to a table to meet with Nicole.

As soon as I made it to the table, Nicole stood up, hugged and kissed me. She contorted her face as she looked behind me. "Who's your friend?"

I glanced back and found the homeless man had followed me.

"Bro! What are you doing?" I said to the man, sternly but confused.

"Oh, I thought we were going on a coffee date," the man explained.

"Man! If you don't get your dusty ass out of here!"

He rolled his eyes and walked out of the coffee shop.

Nicole and I typically meet here every day during my lunch break. She was my new beautiful ebony princess. We had been dating for a few months. We met on a dating app and, at first, she was just a rebound from my breakup with Shontae. She had since graduated to my steady

The dating pool in Las Vegas had pee in it. Dating here was similar to swimming through piles and piles of trash, searching for garbage, and only finding more trash. I am sure women have their complaints about men. Nothing against men, but I think most are untrustworthy, selfish, disgusting, disturbing, and horrible creatures—especially the guys who wear Gucci belts. Never trust a man who has a Gucci belt. Some think they know it all. Some talk too damn much, lie, and steal. Some of these apathetic clowns lack empathy or sympathy. Some perpetrate as if they are rich. Some have money but lack everything else. Some are overly cocky for no reason. Some buy big trucks with oversized tires because they lack in size. But the women are the worst.

A good woman is an investment, but an immature chick is a bill. Sure, you have some women taking care of their business and are financially independent. Some of the women I have met in Vegas are insecure, bad bitch wannabes, part-time fitness models who are Boss bitches without any employees. Some act cuter than they are. Some are not that bright. Some talk too much and also talk with a mouthful of food. Some lack a sense of humor and a personality. They ask too many questions they already know the answers to. Some are emotionally unstable with daddy issues, and others have baby daddy issues. You can identify these types of women because they are usually screaming, 'Men ain't shit.'

Some bring more baggage than what they bring to the table. Some women demand more than their actual value or what they offer. Some want to be the boss and be taken care of. Some are thirst-trapping attention whores with OnlyFans accounts. Some are ambitionless gold-diggers. Some sleep around for free, and others are professional prostitutes. Women say they want an honest man who does not lie, yet they lie every day—heavy makeup covering their face, hair extensions, fake lashes, fake breasts, fake asses, or fake lips. All lies.

Other than Shontae, I'd never struck such gold as I had with Nicole. She was a natural beauty and an intellectual. She believed in me, but most importantly, she believed in us.

As we got settled at the table, Nicole leaned over and asked, "How was work?"

I took a gulp from my drink before I answered, "Uh...I accidentally quit my job today."

Nicole blank stared at me for a few seconds. Suddenly, she erupted into laughter. "You're so silly."

My deadpan response suggested I was serious.

Her laughter faded away. "Did you really quit your job?"

"Yeah, I kind of did. By accident."

"Oh my god! I need you to have a job. I thought we were planning to move in together. What will you do for money? What will I tell my parents?"

"You tell them I'm never getting rich working a nine-to-five."

"I want someone with job security," she said. All of a sudden, Nicole experienced a panic attack that turned into a childlike temper tantrum. She fell dramatically to the ground. "Why won't you men give me what I want?" She screamed and stomped her feet while crossing her arms tightly across her chest. Her lower lip curved out in a pout. "This is so unfair." She said this as she began to cry, her cheeks turning red. "You guys never give me anything I want!" She yelled, drawing stares as she wiped her eyes dramatically, leaving a path of knocked-over napkins on the tables she collided with. "I can't deal with this." Nicole rushed out of the coffee shop.

I looked around in a state of confusion and embarrassment. I watched her pace back and forth in front of the coffee shop, talking to herself, as though she was figuring out what to do or say.

A few awkward moments passed and Nicole re-entered and sat down again.

"I think we need space," Nicole declared.

"Space? What does 'space' consist of?"

"Not dating anymore. I'm not comfortable in this relationship anymore."

"The only way to be comfortable is to be rich."

"I like the idea of becoming rich, but let's be realistic. What if—"

"What if what?"

"What if you never get rich? What if you're never successful? You don't have a degree to fall back on."

"You don't need a college degree to become successful."

"Those self-help books you read are doing more harm than good."

"So those books you read in college are any better? What has your communication degree done for you? Oh, that's right, you're a cocktail waitress for a casino."

"I'm thirty, Terrence. I'm supposed to be married with a mortgage, kids, and a job. My parents already think we can't financially survive together. I want to be comfortable. I want a normal middle-class lifestyle."

"The middle class gets taxed the most yet works the hardest. You're being so manipulated, and you don't even know it. It's a setup for you to die in debt. I'm tired of just surviving. I hate only affording to be broke. Getting paid twenty-six times in a 365-day year cycle does not entice me."

A few moments of unspoken words pass.

"We're not on the same page. Let's just be friends."

"'Let's be friends' as in you want to see other people?"

"Maybe…I don't know."

I take a second to let it sink into my brain. "You and I would've never been if I'd used a condom."

"What!"

"You think I'm a bitch? Do you think I'm going to sit around in a friendship with you? Dancing around emotions and thoughts of what could've been." I stood to my feet. "We will not be friends." This time I dashed off.

Some seconds later, I hurried back over to snatch the drink I bought her and marched out of the coffee shop.

As I left the coffee shop, I handed the bum the drink.

The bum took a sip of the tea. He grimaced at the taste of the drink and spit it out. "Brother-man! This ain't no skinny caffè mocha."

I stopped for a beat and stared at the bum. I did something nice for that guy, and he tried to take advantage of me. How could one still be greedy and ungrateful under such living conditions?

Things could always be worse, I thought as I walked away and carried on with my life. I shuffled through my phone, tapped on the App Store, and re-downloaded all the dating apps. I was now back on the dating market.

CHAPTER 10

Hollywood sat in the investigation room, staring at Agent Thurman, who returned the stare. Defense attorney Sasha Sanchez entered the room and took a seat next to Hollywood.

"Finally!" an annoyed Hollywood said.

Sasha chucked a threatening glare at Hollywood, its intensity instantly subduing him. "Sorry for the delay," a flustered Sasha said, breaking the tension. "I misplaced my purse."

"Now that my lawyer is here. Let's talk. What is all of this about?" Hollywood demanded.

"Your establishment has been flagged under 18 US Code Chapter 25 for counterfeiting and forgery. We've confiscated over one hundred thousand dollars in counterfeit bills. Seventy thousand dollars of counterfeit bills were from last night."

Hollywood pounded his fist on the table. "That con-artist, cocksucking, son of a bitch. I was robbed!"

"I take it you know the source. Do you have a name?"

"No, I don't, but Dallas Houston knows who the guy is. Every Thursday, I host a poker game in the basement of Allure Lounge. Sometimes, I play games with celebrities or professional athletes. But these last few months, that's slowed down. So, I invited local politicians and business owners to play cards. This guy Dallas started to play with me, and he brought another guy along with him. The guy had a shitload of $1 bills in a trash bag. He wanted to exchange them, and so I let him. But I didn't create those bills."

"My client is the victim here," the lawyer confirmed.

"I'm the victim?" Hollywood asked as he turned his head to the lawyer.

The visibly annoyed Sasha nodded her head.

"That's right!" Hollywood shouted spiritedly. "I'm the victim."

Sasha sighed. "You unlawfully arrested Mr. Sanchez for bills that clearly came from an outside source."

"That is correct," Agent Thurman confirmed.

"I demand the immediate release of my client and for all the charges to be dropped."

Agent Thurman nodded her head. "You're free to go, Mr. Sanchez."

"That's it?" asked a baffled Hollywood. He had never gotten out of a pickle with the law this fast.

A visibly irritated Sasha stood and stormed out of the investigation room.

"What a time to be alive?" Hollywood said as he grew smug and celebrated as if he had scored a touchdown.

Moments later, Hollywood caught up with Sasha as they both exited the building. Several beats passed as they walked toward a nearby parking lot.

"I told you it wasn't my fault," said a gloating Hollywood.

"Yeah, not this time."

"What does that mean? I deserve some sympathy. I was the victim."

They reach Sasha's car, a black Mercedes-Benz, and stop walking.

"Hoo-freaking-ray, Jorge! You actually didn't do something you said you didn't do. I'm running for office. I can't risk your reputation disrupting the campaign. So, get all of your fuck-ups out now. You'll be back to being our parents' liability," Sasha said, as she got in her vehicle and slammed the door.

"Are you firing me?"

"Call it whatever the hell you'd like!"

"You know what…you're fired," said Hollywood. "I'll never ask you for another thing."

Sasha flipped Hollywood the bird, reversed her car, and sped out of the parking lot.

CHAPTER 11

A few blocks away from the coffee shop was a bank. Who would have thought I would be casing a bank to rob? But I could not even get a cash advance from a payday loan. Desperate measures call for desperate actions. As I approached the entrance, someone bumped into me. "Sorry about that," I said.

"Open your eyes," the man said.

"Fuck you," I responded. "I apologized to you."

Another man was standing behind the guy that I bumped into. I could not see his face until he stood side-by-side the man I had cursed at.

"Look what the wind blew in," said Reverend Hillman dressed in an impeccably tailored, expensive navy-blue suit.

"You know this person?" the man asked.

Reverend Hillman stared down at my feet and noticed a missing shoe. He chuckled as he shook his head with disgust. "Unfortunately I do, Dallas. He's an old friend of the family. Nice seeing you again, Terrence," Reverend Hillman said as they walked off and continued with their conversation.

The last time he and I were together was when Shontae and I were together. It was a little over a year ago. Shontae, her mother, Louise, her father, Reverend Hillman, and I were finishing dinner. Victor was at the table as well. Reverend Hillman invited Victor over for Thanksgiving.

I was aware that Reverend Hillman had set Shontae up on dates behind my back, but never before had he so blatantly tried to set her up with Victor right in front of my face. He was very fond of Victor.

Anytime Reverend Hillman looked in Victor's direction, he would smile with his eyes. Victor was the son he never had. And because he never had a son, he wanted his only daughter to marry the guy he approved of. But I was the one his daughter had eyes for.

Reverend Hillman frowned at me whenever his eyes floated my way. Though I was used to his dirty stares, this particular glare was different from all of the other looks he shot in my direction. This time it appeared as if he wanted to fight. Everyone at the dinner table felt his energy toward me. So, I addressed it. I remember asking, "Is there a problem, sir?"

"Let's talk," said Reverend Hillman.

"Not now, Daddy," Shontae pleaded.

"We'll only be a few seconds."

We got up from the table and moved to the living room.

"What are your intentions?" the reverend asked.

"Mr. Hillman—"

"That's Reverend Hillman," he said, correcting me.

"Sorry… Reverend Hillman, my intentions are genuine. I have ambitions of marrying your daughter."

"Okay, so what's your pitch?"

"My pitch?"

"Yes, an ambitious man should always have a pitch."

"I plan to start a business one day."

"But you have no degree."

"Respectfully, sir, I don't need a degree to become a business owner."

"You need a business first," Reverend Hillman said. "How much money do you make a month? A more direct question: Can you even take care of your mother?"

"Excuse me. What does my mother have to do with this?"

"If you can't take care of your mother, how do you expect to take care of my daughter? You're no doctor or lawyer. What's your credit score?"

"What does a credit score have to do with me marrying your daughter?"

"How will I benefit from you marrying my daughter?"

"Why are you trying to leverage your daughter?"

"Are you who you believe you are?"

I thought about it for a minute and replied, "Um, yes."

"I don't believe you. Respectfully, you're not economically ready to be a part of this family. I'm sorry. I disapprove of you."

Reverend Hillman walked off and rejoined his family at the table. He placed his arm around Victor and the two began to yuk it up. I stood deflated, before leaving deep in my thoughts. I will never forget how he made me feel, but he was right. I was not able to take care of his daughter.

I still felt defeated as I gazed over at the arrogant reverend approaching an intersection. Reverend Hillman crossed the street, made eye contact with me, shook his head, and resumed his conversation with Mr. Houston.

"OK, bet!" I mumbled to myself as I nodded with conviction. One day, I'd prove him wrong, even if I was unsure it would happen that day. He was the only reason I broke up with Shontae and why I was in front of a bank with the intention of robbing it.

I entered the lobby of the bank and started to wander around. I have watched bank robbery films like *Dog Day Afternoon*, *Set it Off*, *Heat*, and *Public Enemies*. Most of those characters were arrested or died in the movie; a very low success rate, in other words.

A banking assistant approached me. "Can I help you with something, sir?"

"I'm just browsing."

My response slightly threw off the banking assistant. But I decided to exit the bank because the risk did not match the reward, and simply put, I did not have a budget to rob a bank.

CHAPTER 12

Brandon approached a shopping plaza. The plaza had a few boutique stores, trendy restaurants, a nail salon, and a hair salon right next to it. He walked up to Style & Grace Hair Gallery and placed his face across the window to look inside. He noticed Emily sitting in the stylist's chair.

Emily and a few of her bridesmaids were getting their hair done in preparation for their bachelorette party. They were only a few days away from Emily's wedding.

Brandon pushed open the salon's glass door, the cold blast of air conditioning providing a brief reprieve from the warm desert spring day.

Inside, the salon had a stylish mix of modern designs with sleek, black seats flanking the walls, each with a smiling guest facing a large mirror. The scent of hair products and the gentle hum of blow dryers filled the air.

Brandon was greeted with smiles as he scanned the salon. He was struck by the salon's upbeat and happy atmosphere. He noticed team members working together and conversing with clients while beautiful hair was being styled.

All of the stylists were dressed in black, their hair and makeup flawless, and two stylists worked on clients simultaneously. The banter between clients and stylists, combined with calm background music, created a buzz of energy that was both comforting and exhilarating. The friendly atmosphere was reminiscent of the TV show *Cheers*, but rather than a bar, it was a hair salon where everyone knew your name.

"Hi, welcome," said the receptionist up front.

Brandon gave a head nod as he tiptoed over to Emily and snuck behind her.

Emily had to take a double glance at the mirror before realizing it was Brandon. She jumped to her feet, and they hugged. "Oh my God, Brandon! You made it. I assumed you weren't going to be able to come."

"I wouldn't have missed my baby sister's wedding for the world."

"How did you know I was here?"

"Oh," Brandon said as he began scratching the back of his head. "I had your location in my phone."

"But I never sent my location."

"Well…yeah…about that. So…Karla and I kind of started dating."

Emily's jaw dropped. "You and Karla date?"

"Well…yes. I think. I hope. I'm not sure all the way. But we went out on a date one night. And when she left to use the restroom, I sort of went through her purse, grabbed her phone, and texted her location to me without realizing it was your phone."

"That's creepy work, Brandon. But yeah, I left my phone at work one day, and she promised to bring it to me after her date. I didn't think the date was with you, though," Emily said with a giggle.

"What's wrong with me?"

"I guess I didn't think you were her type."

"What is her type?"

"Karla is a good woman. I don't want you to ruin her. She has a bright future ahead of her.

"A woman like Karla could help get me on track. Who knows? If she acts right, she could be your sister-in-law one day."

"Ok. We shall see about that," Emily said. "Have you talked to Dad?"

"Uh…no, not really," Brandon said. "He doesn't like me all too much these days."

"I mean, you stole and wrecked his car. Not to mention the other things he did, bailing you out of trouble."

"Am I not allowed to evolve?"

"You most certainly are entitled to evolve," Emily said with a chuckle.

"Whose all with you?"

Emily pointed as she counted three ladies in the chair having their hair done. "It's just the five of us."

Brandon's face contorted from confusion. "But I only see four of you."

Emily rubbed her stomach.

Brandon's eyes widened as pure excitement rushed through him. "Are you serious?"

"Yep! You're going to be an uncle soon."

"Wow! I'm so happy for you both. We need to celebrate."

"Um, Brandon. We're already celebrating. It's my bachelorette party."

"Oh, yeah. That's right. Okay, cool. Well, I'm paying for everyone's hair today."

All of the clients at the salon erupted in cheers.

Emily leaned over. "Brandon," she whispered. "That's very generous of you, but can you afford that?"

"Of course, I can. Why would I offer if I couldn't?

"As long as you don't use fake dollar bills, I am fine with however you pay," Emily said.

Brandon's face tensed up. "Fake dollar bill? Why would you say something silly like that?"

"Oh, you haven't heard?"

Brandon shook his head.

"Hollywood was arrested for counterfeiting earlier today. I suppose he has been printing fake dollar bills out of his club. It happened right in front of my face."

"Oh, wow," Brandon said, not surprised. "So, I guess justice was served," he added with a nervous laugh. "It's a good thing I was paying with the money I won from poker," Brandon said, forcing a tight smile.

"Thank you, Brandon. I need to get back to getting my hair done. You boys don't get into too much trouble."

"Oh, we will," Brandon said with a mischievous smile. Emily and Brandon embraced each other for one last hug, and she returned to the stylist chair.

Brandon strolled over to the receptionist.

"I'm paying for all of the ladies in chairs today."

Brandon reached inside his newly acquired fancy bag and pulled out several hundred dollars of real cash that he had converted from counterfeit dollar bills. He handed it over to the receptionist. Brandon paid for every person seated in a stylist's chair, tipped generously, and departed the salon.

CHAPTER 13

The ride home was short, but it felt long after the day I had as I drove along the busy downtown roads. Right as I reached down to turn on some music to drown out the mundane silence, the phone rang.

"You have a collect call from a federal correctional inmate named Charles. Do you accept the charges?" the automated operator said. "Respond 'yes' to accept or 'no' to end this call."

"Yes," I said. A couple of moments passed before the call connected.

"Hey, son," Charles said.

"Dad, what's going on?"

"You have to get your mother out of town."

"Why?

"I got us into a little bind, and I think he's coming for her."

"Who is he?"

"I went into business with this psychopath angel investor and loan shark friend of mine. He is notorious for preying on the desperate. He said if I missed one payment, he'd murder me, you, and your mother."

"How sure are you that he's coming for us?"

"Because he said, 'I'll murder the shit out of you, your wife, and your son.' When I got locked up, the IRS froze all of my accounts. I haven't had a chance to make any payments."

"Mom said all we need is three grand, and we're in the clear."

"Three thousand," he said with an uneasy chuckle. "I wish. It's thirty grand. I've missed a few payments."

"Thirty grand? Do you think I have thirty grand lying around? Can't you talk to him?"

"I've tried. This guy doesn't want to talk anymore. He wants his money and he will use violence as a tool to reinforce his point. If you can't get the money, I recommend that you and your mom skip town for a few years."

"Get off the phone, bitch," another inmate yelled from a distance.

"Yes, sir!" a scared Charles said. "I have to go, son." The phone call ended.

As I approached an intersection and a shopping plaza to my right, a car from the outbound lane abruptly cut me off. I politely blasted the shit out of my horn for several seconds and the lady driving the vehicle flipped me off. I decided to follow her into the plaza.

The lady found a place to park but hesitated to exit her vehicle. I was not sure if she was gathering her stuff to enter the store or was hesitant to exit because I was circling her car like a shark in the ocean.

I found a parking spot several rows away to allow the lady some space to get out of her car and enter the store. From afar, the curly-haired lady was super cute. But cute will not cut it today, as she was about to learn from dealing with me today.

I entered the grocery store and noticed the lady in the produce area. I make my way over to where she was browsing. "Excuse me. Hi, I'm Terrence."

"I'm Cynthia."

"You cut me off a moment ago and then flipped me off. That wasn't polite."

"Oh, you were the one driving that slow-ass beamer?"

"Uh, I was going the speed limit, and you didn't have the right of way."

"Whatever," she said, dismissing me.

"So, you're not going to apologize." She ignored me and went on her way as if she had done nothing. "Okay, bet."

I stormed over to the condiment aisle and grabbed ketchup and mustard. Something familiar caught my eye. I slowed down to get a better glimpse of the familiar face. It was Shontae, who was shopping on the same aisle, but she did not see me as she loaded groceries into her basket. I snuck up from behind.

"Hey!"

"My God! Terrence! Why do you always have to do that?" she said with a giggle.

I missed her giggle, her smile, and just about everything else about her. "Two days in a row, huh? Is that a sign?"

"Almost feels like you're stalking me."

"You're not that important. I lost a bet trying to avoid you."

"Important enough to bet that you wouldn't see me again, but not important enough for you to fight to stay with me?"

"Shontae, I wasn't rich. I couldn't take care of you."

"I'm not a child, and who cares if you weren't rich? Dreamers run the world, Terrence. I believed in you. I believed in us, and you left me."

"I shouldn't have let your father get in my head."

"No, you shouldn't have, and you did, and now, I'm in a relationship."

"There is something I need to tell you about your boy."

Victor approached from behind. Victor looked over at Shontae a few awkward moments, then gazed back over at me. "Can we speak in private?"

Shontae wandered off.

"So, you and Shontae had something in the past. Get over it. I'm working that late-night shift now," Victor said, before walking off. He stopped mid-step and approached me again. "I almost forgot. You left this behind at the office." Victor handed me the old ATM receipt with a negative balance of -$7.39. "It's beyond your budget to be disrespectful. Oh, and thanks for the promotion, homey. I ended up getting promoted to the position you were supposed to get." The smug Victor cracked a smile, patted me on the back, and strode over toward the checkout lanes where Shontae waited.

As I made my way to the self-checkout lane, I noticed Victor mad dogging me. I matched his glare, but I cracked a smile. Hopefully, he knew that this was far from over. I exited the store and walked over to the woman's car that had cut me off earlier and began to decorate it with ketchup and mustard as if it were a Coney Island dog.

CHAPTER 14

The neon lights in Las Vegas pulsated like the city's own heartbeat, casting sweeping shadows as nightfall relieved daytime of its duty. Brandon maneuvered through the packed streets, his mind racing with a well-devised strategy. His heart hammered in his chest as he approached the inconspicuous murky structure located a few blocks away from Downtown Las Vegas.

Brandon was ready to confront Lorenzo Carlucci, one of the city's most notorious loan sharks. Brandon had fallen into Lorenzo's trap months earlier, borrowing money to pay off other gambling obligations. The interest had accumulated faster than Brandon could handle, and now, with his back against the wall, he had turned to desperate measures, which led him to creating counterfeit one-dollar bills. He had spent hours refining the fake dollar bills, assuring they would fool even the most discerning eye. Tonight was the night Brandon was going to pay off his debt and get away scot-free.

Inside, the building was dimly lit and carefully decorated, giving off an aura of danger. Brandon made his way to the back room where

Lorenzo was handling business. Two hefty guards flanked the door, casting suspicious glances at Brandon.

One grumbled, opening the door just enough for Brandon to pass through.

Lorenzo sat behind a massive oak desk, the light from an overhead lamp throwing looming shadows across his face. His head popped up as Brandon entered, and a vulturine grin grew over Lorenzo's lips.

"Brandon, my boy," said Lorenzo with a welcoming yet pleasant tone, albeit with a splash of underlying threat. "I wasn't sure you'd make it back here alive."

Brandon attempted to grin, his palms trembling as he gripped the bag containing the counterfeit money. "I kept my word, Lorenzo. I got your money."

Lorenzo reclined back in his chair and motioned for Brandon to approach. "Let's see it then."

Brandon took a deep breath, walked forward, and placed the bag on Lorenzo's desk. His hands shook slightly as he unclasped it, showing piles of neatly placed $1 bills.

Lorenzo's face contorted as his eyes bucked. "Well, you've been busy," Lorenzo commented, reaching for the cash. He picked up a stack and fanned the bills with a practiced hand. "What's with all the one-dollar bills?"

"Money is money, right?" Brandon said.

As a businessman, Lorenzo could not help but nod in agreement.

"Every last dollar I owe you plus the interest is in that bag," Brandon said, his voice firm despite the adrenaline rushing through his veins.

Lorenzo continued to examine the money, his eyes narrowing slightly but not giving any signs of suspicion. "You know what, Brandon? I was beginning to worry you may try to skip town. But, even if it's a shit ton on one-dollar bills, I commend you for this."

Brandon gulped hard and maintained eye contact. "I promised you I would repay every dollar. I just needed time."

Lorenzo nodded with satisfaction. He zipped the bag and laid it aside. "Consider your debt paid. But always remember, Brandon, if you ever need another loan, I am your guy."

Brandon faked another smile as relief washed over him. "Thank you, Lorenzo. I appreciate it."

Lorenzo waved him off. "Now, get the fuck out of here and enjoy your freedom."

Brandon did not need to be warned twice. He turned and left the room, his heart still hammering. The guards gave him one last stern look before allowing him to pass. As he went outside, he felt a weight lift off his shoulders. He had done it. He had repaid his debt and had walked away unharmed.

But as he made his way through the crowd, Brandon realized this was not over. If Lorenzo ever found out those bills were fake, there would be hell to pay. For the time being, he allowed himself a moment of victory. He had outsmarted one of Las Vegas's most dangerous villains, and he planned to make the most of his second opportunity.

The city lights blurred past him as he drove away from the building. Brandon had taken a great risk, but, tonight, luck was on his side. Now it was up to him to keep ahead of the game and guarantee that his luck would never run out.

CHAPTER 15

I *finally made it home. What a horrible day?!* I thought as I stormed through the condo. I lost out on a promotion because I quit a job, I thought I was being laid off from. And subsequently, the guy who was with my Shontae got the raise intended for me. I even stepped in human shit. Why could it not just be dog poop I stepped in?

I took a seat on the couch and grabbed a *Homes and Land* magazine that Justice liked to keep on the coffee table in the living room. I flicked through the pages, studying beautiful homes that were in some of my dream neighborhoods around the Las Vegas metro. I came across one that caught my eye. It was a $2 million home overlooking Green Valley in Henderson.

I closed my eyes and tried to envision myself in this house. But the sounds of a squeaky bed and a woman moaning in the background disrupted my manifestation attempt. At least one of us was having a good day.

I checked all of my freshly redownloaded dating apps. I swiped left and right until I ran out of swipes. Once I finished swiping, I checked my matches and messages from Tinder, Hinge, and Bumble. I noticed a few new connections. Some of the profiles on the apps were fake, some were unattractive, and I disconnected with them immediately.

I liked a couple of profiles, and I scrolled through the pictures to get a better idea. There was one profile that caught my eye. Her profile name was LesFit. I shuffled through her photos to see more of her. She appeared to be a fitness model, which was not unusual for someone living in Vegas. There were pictures of her shooting guns at a firing range and some of her hiking in the mountains. She appeared to be into sports because there was another picture of her in Las Vegas Raider gear at the Allegiant Stadium. I typed a message to her: *Hey, I am Terrence. You're my kind of cute.* I sent an emoji with the hearts as eyes.

Several moments passed as the bed continued squeaking in the background. LesFit responded: *Hey, Terrence, I like your pictures. All except for the bathroom mirror selfie ones with your shirt off.* She added a smiley face.

I responded: *LOL! Would you like to meet up for a drink and get to know each other better in person?*

A half-dressed, frantic Justice rushed out from the back of the condo several moments later.

"Thank God! I thought you were someone else," Justice said with a sigh of relief as he gazed down at my feet. "Uh, where the hell is your other shoe?"

"It's been one of those days. I'd rather not talk about it."

Justice attempted to conceal his laughter. Suddenly, a striking hourglass-frame mamacita in Lululemon gym attire popped out of the bedroom. She rushed to Justice, kissed him, and skated out of the condo.

"Was that the little red dress from last night?"

Justice nodded. "Her name is Karla," Justice said as he walked toward the refrigerator. "I'm calling off the wedding. So, you're going to have to break the news to everyone."

"Nope! You're on your own, my boy."

"You're the best man. That's your job."

"Nope! My tasks as the best man consist of setting up the bachelor party, which, by the way, I can't afford to fund or participate in, making a toast at the wedding, and smashing a bridesmaid."

Justice grabbed a bottle of cognac and two shot glasses off the granite kitchen countertop. He moved over to the couch. "I can't go on with this lie. But I will make it known after the weekend. I plan to sleep with as many women as I can until it is completely out of my system, and, if it's not, I'll decide to end the whole thing."

"I hope that works out for you."

"But I needed to talk to you about our living arrangements."

"Oh yeah. About that…I was planning to move in with Nicole, but we broke up today."

"Damn! What happened?"

"I kind of quit my job and she was not happy with my decision, so she thought it would be best that she and I be friends."

"You lost your girl, your job, and a shoe all in the same day. That's funny," Justice said with a chuckle.

"What is so funny about that, Justice?"

"Nothing," Justice said as he tried to conceal his laughter.

The door flew open, and I jumped to my feet in fight-or-flight mode. Unfortunately, my day just got worse. It was Brandon barging through the door unannounced with an expensive designer purse draped over his shoulder.

"Is that my future brother-in-law?" Brandon said.

Justice stood and greeted his old buddy. "Bro! Why are you carrying a purse?" asked Justice.

"I found it," Brandon said defensively.

A confused Justice stared at me for a few moments before returning his gaze back to Brandon. "Where did you randomly find an expensive designer bag?"

Brandon continued, "I found this unlocked car in the parking lot and—"

"Committed grand theft larceny," I said interjecting.

"If you leave a Birkin bag in an unsecured car, that, my friend, is a blessing where I'm from," Brandon said, justifying his position.

"No, we don't, fool! We call that shit stealing."

"Terrence, this all kinda started as an A and B conversation, so, you can C your way out before D jumps over E and Fs' you up like a G."

"Don't let the alphabet get you're A-S-S beat," I said.

"Easy, Terrence. Happy to see you, too." Brandon dug in his pocket. "I also found these," Brandon said as he opened up his hand and revealed three pills.

Justice's phone rang. He pulled it out only to ignore it. He instead grabbed a pill and examined it. "What's this?"

"It's Molly. This girl I met on Tinder gave them to me. She gave me the pills, told me to find two other friends, and get on their level. They're rolling on Molly, baby. They're trying to hook up."

Justice placed a pill in his mouth. He grabbed another pill, broke it down, and put it in a shot glass full of cognac.

"You got pills from a girl you don't know. And now you want me to take it?" I asked.

Brandon soaked in the questions for a second. "Yeah."

"You're out of your rabbit-ass mind. I got other shit to do."

I reached for my glass and downed it.

"Terrence, that was the wrong glass," Justice said.

Suddenly, I felt a little woozy.

CHAPTER 16

We started off driving down Las Vegas Boulevard. The music that blared in the car hit differently. Or maybe it was the wind that blew across my face as my head hung out of the car window. The air felt fantastic. At that moment, I understood why dogs loved sticking their heads out of car windows. It felt so amazing. Suddenly, we reached a stoplight, and Brandon jumped on the hood and started doing some random twerking in the middle of the intersection.

The next thing I remembered was petting this huge friendly gold lion. I had never been this close to one. A few shots later, we blacked out. The next thing I saw was Brandon who sat on the nose of the fake ass Sphinx. And somehow, we were on a roller coaster in New York City.

We took a few more shots at the top of the Eiffel Tower, where we met up with some ladies. One of them was a voluptuous big, beautiful woman named Becca. We took a few more shots, before ending up back on the Strip in a big, lovely pond with an impeccable sprinkler system.

We took a few more shots on this slow-ass Ferris wheel, which they call the High Roller.

"SHOTS! SHOTS! SHOTS! SHOTS!" Brandon yelled.

And the rest of these fools started yelling, "SHOTS! SHOTS! SHOTS! SHOTS!" As you may have predicted, we took more shots.

We were at a bar, drinking at a sportsbook. Brandon was at the window placing bets, and Justice was talking to all three of the women who joined up. So, I guess, we are not all drinking at the bar. It is only I who drinks at the bar.

"Another one, please," I signaled to the bartender.

As we walked down the Strip, Justice talked with two of the ladies. My hooker-meter for spotting prostitutes was off. The molly-infused concoction clouded my judgment. The ladies were beautiful, yet not as dolled up as your typical call girl. They were extra flirty and friendly. We took shots in Julius Caesars's house near the sportsbook, and these chicks started making out with each other.

I saw one of the women stuffing some random guy's face in her chest, and the other sneaked the guy's wallet out of his back pocket. I was too far gone to say anything.

We took more shots at this cigar bar and…"Hold up!" I said as I sobered up for a minute. "Who in the hell is paying for all of these damn shots?"

"Enjoy yourself, my boy," Brandon slurred to me. "It's all on me."

And everything blacked out once again.

We were now on the sidewalk of the Strip. Becca pushed Brandon and me along the way in a red Target shopping cart. I'm not sure how a Target shopping cart made it to the Strip because there was not a Target nearby. I am also unsure how I got into it, but tonight, we were about that life. Not sure if I was tweaking, but the couple across the way looked familiar. Yep. It was who I thought it was. Victor walked on the other side of the street with my beautiful Shontae.

Some embarrassing blacked-out moments later, I was pissing in a sink next to a lady who was trying to wash her hands. Justice joined me as he started to piss next to the lady. The disgusted lady hurried away, and Brandon took her place between us. Brandon lifted his leg up like a male dog would and started peeing on the mirror.

Now we were in a mall. It felt like I was wearing new clothes. Justice was not wearing the same clothes he had on earlier, and Brandon was in a black suit.

We drank near a fancy sportsbook at another bar with some beach that had a club on it. Brandon placed another bet at the window, and Justice started making out with one of the ladies as the other groped Justice while sneaking his wallet out of his back pocket. So yet again, we were not all drinking at the bar. It was me who was the only one drinking at the bar.

We ended up on what is called the Big Shot. I might have taken too many shots. I have lived in Vegas my whole life, and I had never seen a town like this. But you will see a city differently when you are 921 feet above the ground. Forty-five miles per hour later, we were at 1,081 feet, Brandon and Justice giggling like school kids. By the time we reached the bottom, the once-laughing Justice started puking all over himself. Brandon appeared to be in tears.

Several hours later, we entered some random party full of naked people. I sent a text message to Justice: *What do we do?*

Justice responded: *Don't act too normal. We have to fit in.*

Suddenly, Brandon got buck-ass nude and decided to run around in the chaos. Justice, unable to resist the urge, slowly ripped off the rest of his clothes. I attempted to pull off my shirt but decided to take a nap on the ground.

CHAPTER 17

Several hours had passed. I woke on the floor next to one of the beds in what appeared to be a hotel room. Adjacent to my face was what appeared to be vomit. I was still wearing everything I had on the night before. Justice was asleep on the chair in the seating area where there was a large, high-definition TV. I walked to the window to see the view of the Las Vegas Strip as the sun rose. The suite was plush with everything you thought a world-class resort on the Strip should have. I tiptoed to the bathroom. I noticed a jetted tub, a large separate glass shower with two showerheads, and a seating area. I looked in the mirror and noticed the blazer I was wearing. I took it off and saw the tags read Gucci. Everything I was wearing was Gucci. The shoes were Gucci and also the belt. Even though I liked it, I still don't trust anybody with a Gucci belt. I exited the bathroom.

In the bed lay Becca, who was on top of what appeared to be Brandon. Suddenly, the lady let out a violent, thunderous fart that awakened everyone in the room. Brandon's feet started to wiggle from under her. Becca woke up and rushed out of bed and out of the hotel suite.

"I didn't hit that, did I?" Brandon asked.

Justice scrolled through his phone. "That's what the videos and pictures in my phone say. But don't feel bad. Terrence hit it, too."

A small amount of vomit came out of my mouth as I redirected myself back to the bathroom and puked some more of my brains out. I recovered and made my way over to the sink to wash my hands. I splashed cold water on my face to get the sleep out of my eye.

Seconds later, in walked Brandon. "What's up, big dog?"

Brandon headed straight for the toilet and started to pee. I stopped what I was doing and watched his reflection in the mirror with disbelief. Brandon flushed the toilet and strutted out of the bathroom.

We were passed out longer than I'd thought because it was not morning. It was closer to sunset. Brandon made his way over to the seating area where Justice sat.

I followed right behind. "Don't you ever walk into another room I'm in, nasty ass little boy," I said firmly.

"It's not like you were naked," Brandon said. "You weren't even using the toilet, and I had to pee."

"Justice, check your boy. And he didn't wash his hands, either."

"Bro, you should feel comfortable around me now. I've seen you naked."

"What the hell are you talking about?"

"Remember, last night. We had sex together."

"I don't remember."

Justice pulled out his phone and showed me a video of me running naked and being chased by Becca.

There was an awkward pause as Brandon noticeably started to scratch at his groin area.

"The same hands he is scratching himself with, are the same hands he didn't wash by the way," I said as I disgustingly watched Brandon.

"You need to get checked out," said Justice.

"I guess I shouldn't have slept with your mom last night. I'm joking. I think that big girl might have given me something."

"You didn't use a condom?" I asked.

Justice scrolled through his phone and found a piece of visual evidence. "After further review, the ruling on the field has been confirmed. Brandon did not use a prophylactic."

Brandon continued to scratch himself. "I was drunk and rolling on Molly."

"That's so damn disgusting."

"You hit it, too."

"I used a condom, though."

"How do you know?"

"I'm still wearing it, fool."

"So, you are aware that you hit it, too."

A small amount of regurgitation enters my mouth. I cannot believe I ran a train with Brandon.

Justice started to pat his pockets. "Have you guys seen my wallet?

My eyes widen as I stared at Brandon.

"It wasn't me. I can't find mine either. It must have been those damn girls from last night."

"We're too old to be doing dumb shit," I said as my phone lit up. I did not want to look at it yet. Brandon grabbed the phone off the table and stared at the screensaver.

"Is this your lady in the picture, T? She's hot, bro. Oh my God! I love cougars," said Brandon.

I snatched the phone from Brandon's hand and slammed it on the table. "That's not a cougar. That's my mama, fool."

Brandon picked up the phone off the table and studied the screensaver. "Oh right! That is Mrs. Ware. Damn! Your mother is still fine!"

"Wow. Brandon just said he'd bang your mom," Justice said.

"I didn't say I'd bang his mom," Brandon said as he grabbed the phone and gave it one more glance. "But if the opportunity presented itself, I'm not saying I wouldn't bang her."

I lunged forward and grabbed Brandon by the throat. Justice attempted to pull me off, preventing me from committing manslaughter.

"What's your deal?"

"Don't disrespect the woman that birthed me."

"It's a joke. I'd never sleep with a friend's mom."

"We're not friends," I affirmed.

Brandon pulled out a thick knot of $1 bills from the designer bag and proceeded to "make it rain" on me.

"Not again! Another asshole done 'Made it Rain' on me," I said as I went into full predator mode, but Justice got in between us.

"Woah! Wait! What's with this guy? It's a peace offering, Terrence. You don't like money?"

"Money doesn't like me right now," I said as I tried to calm myself down. I took a seat. "How in the hell did I get dipped in Gucci anyway?"

A sinister grin slapped across Brandon's face as he stood proud right before answering, "Because I make dollar bills, my boys."

"I get that," Justice said. "But how?"

"I made dollar bills."

"Yeah, but how?" I asked. "Your boy kind of needs some insight."

"I make them," said Brandon.

"Yeah, but how, fool?"

"By making the bills."

"Brandon! I need fast cash. How did you make the bills? My parents are in the middle of a crisis and I'm desperate."

"I literally make them."

I eyed Brandon down for a few seconds before going all the way hell off on him. "I'm trying to have as much patience with you as I humanly can—"

"Terrence! I make $1 bills. Like, I printed them out myself one by one."

"Counterfeiting! Got it! That's all you had to say," I said. "But…uh… you know you're going to jail, right?"

Brandon shushed and whispered, "Not so loud." He pulled out another thick knot from the purse and tossed it over to Justice. "Pretty legit, huh?"

Justice flipped through the wad of $1 bills. "What gave you the idea to make these?"

"I went to YouTube University, typed in how to make money, then clicked on the first video that popped up."

I shook my head in disbelief. You can find out how to do anything on YouTube.

"Can you print out bigger bills?" asked Justice.

"Yeah, but it is too risky. People check big bills for counterfeiting. They never check one-dollar bills for authenticity."

"He's right. Kinda ingenious," Justice said. "How much did you print out?"

"I lost count after two hundred grand," Brandon said.

"You have two hundred grand in fake bills?"

"Nope! I have more."

Justice and I locked eyes. Brandon created another get-rich-quick scheme, and I kind of liked it. The American dollar is not backed by gold or any other natural resource, so I didn't see anything wrong with it in that moment.

"What are you planning to do with the rest of the counterfeit bills?" Justice asked.

"Exchange them into real capital. I've been using the fake ones to exchange them for real bills in underground poker games and other places that accept cash."

There were a lot of things I could do with a little bit of the money Brandon created. "I hate to be that guy, Brandon," I said. "But…uh…if you don't let me in, I'm snitching."

"I wouldn't have told you about it if I didn't plan to split it," said Brandon.

"I say we spread the rest of the bills equally," Justice suggested. "We convert it to real cash, invest it, and whoever becomes a millionaire first, takes the losers' possessions. That includes any properties, assets, cars, and whatever is in the loser's bank account."

"That sounds like Monopoly. Did you forget what happened the last time we all played Monopoly?" Brandon said with a chuckle.

Justice and I grew silent as tension slid in between us, reflecting on an old Monopoly battle.

"Justice is a sore loser."

"You cheated."

"How? You just couldn't count."

"We were kids, Terrence. Get over it."

"Admit I won fair and square and we're good, Justice."

A pouty Justice and I crossed our arms simultaneously as a few brief tense moments of silence creeped into the room. It took several moments before the tension dissipated.

"Whatever," I said, breaking the tension. "Back to the real fake ass money. Aren't you afraid of leaving behind a paper trail for someone to find?"

"Like who, Terrence?"

"Uh, like the feds, fool!"

"Oh, I have a plan."

"Really!?" I said. "You can barely walk and talk at the same time. But please tell me about the last plan that worked out for you."

"Not too long ago, before printing off the bills, I got fired from my job at the mortuary, so that I could draw unemployment. Take that to the bank for a plan."

"How did you get fired?" a curious Justice asked.

"A dead body came up missing and they blamed me for it."

Justice gave me a disturbed look. "Okay! So, let's get back to business. Let's make it more of a gentlemen's bet so business does not get too personal whenever I win. We'll take only half of the losers' assets. But also, the losers must bow down to the winner whenever said winner enters a room until the losers become a millionaire. It doesn't matter whether we're at a restaurant, a grocery store, or anywhere in between, the loser must make an effort to bow. No explanations for why you're bowing, and if asked, you must reply only with "He is my king. I'm not worthy!"

"What happens in the case one or all of us become millionaires at the same time?" Brandon asked.

"I highly doubt that'll happen," Justice said smugly. "But if that were to be the case that one or more of us become millionaires at the same time, it will come down to big bank taking little bank. Whoever has the highest net worth, wins the bet."

A chuckling Brandon extended his hand to shake on the bet. "Okay, bet. I'm in."

I was a little hesitant, but what else did I have to lose? "Bet. Let's do it." We all shook on it except I with Brandon. I needed not to touch his nasty ass hands.

"Now! Let's blow off some steam," Justice suggested. "You guys want to kick off my bachelor party at the strip club?"

"Not really," I said. "Strippers are walking, talking, buck-ass nude petri dishes. It's almost equivalent to sitting bare ass on a public toilet seat."

"I know a place better than any strip club," said Brandon. "It's a gay bar right off the strip called Taste of Rainbow."

"I've heard there are a lot of women at gay bars," Justice confirmed. "I'm talking smoking hot women."

"Yeah, but some of them might not be women," I said.

"The cool part is that you guys are good-looking. You might even get free drinks, if you're lucky." Brandon received an alert on his phone. He checked it. "I have something to do. The suite is booked for the week. I'll meet you guys back here later." Brandon hustled out of the suite.

"Wanna go to that bar Brandon recommended?"

"Nope."

"Why? Are you homophobic?"

"No! If I were a woman, I'd be a lesbian. And I appreciate gay men because their efforts quadruple the number of women in my life. But why would we leave the Strip? There are tourists everywhere with the mindset that whatever happens in Vegas stays in Vegas. I really wanna exploit that."

"What if there are a lot of hot women there?" Justice said.

"What if my mother had balls? She'd probably be my father."

"I'm going. Stay here and jerk yourself off for all I care."

"Great! This place should have some fancy lotion somewhere."

"At least go with me," Justice pleaded. "If it's not popping, we'll come back. The Strip is not going anywhere."

"Rock, Paper, Scissors. If I win, we stay on the Strip. If you win, we go to the spot Brandon recommended."

"Okay, on three."

I nodded. Shaking my head hurt from all of the shots we took the previous night.

"One, Two, Three, Shoot."

Justice threw a rock, and I threw out scissors.

"I always beat you," said a smug Justice.

"Except in Monopoly."

We stared each other down for a few moments. That old Monopoly game was still a touchy subject.

CHAPTER 18

No words were spoken between Brandon and Mr. Houston as they rode along in the plastic-wrapped backseat of a dark-tinted stretch Lincoln Town Car. Brandon slid on a pair of gloves. A couple of moments passed as the uneasy Brandon stared at a stoic Mr. Houston.

"Something wrong with your eyes?" Mr. Houston said sternly.

"I'm tired of doing your dirty work," Brandon responded with apprehension.

"I was supposed to win that hand. You won when the instructions were for me to win. So, until your debt is settled, you're my bitch, and you'll get fuck however I like."

The vehicle slowed to a complete stop. Mr. Houston kicked open the door.

Hollywood entered the limo. Brandon immediately became uncomfortable.

"You con artist, cocksucking, son of a bitch. You robbed me," Hollywood shouted at Brandon as he dove at him.

"I don't know what you're talking about, sir. I won fair and square."

"You know what I meant. Those fake dollar bills you brought into my club."

"Everyone, calm down." Mr. Houston said. "You get into my vehicle and don't speak to me?"

"I'm sorry. How are you, Dallas?"

"How am I?" Mr. Houston said as he pulled off his glasses. Mr. Houston tossed over an envelope of photos onto Hollywood's lap. A few uncanny moments passed as Hollywood opened the envelope and scanned through the photos. Mr. Houston slid down an armrest, pulled out a pair of Isotoner gloves from the compartment, and slid his fingers through them. He pulled out a pistol and handed the gun to Brandon. Brandon timidly grabbed the gun with his index finger and thumb, slowly raised it, and trained it on Hollywood.

"This has to be a misunderstanding," said Hollywood as he grew uncomfortable. "I can explain."

"Did you know that I know how much you make and every single penny you've spent? I have access to your financial records. And it has come to my knowledge that you've been sleeping with my wife."

"Maybe we can work something out," Hollywood said.

"She sure is a hot piece of ass. Isn't that what you said?" Mr. Houston recalled.

"Look, Dallas, I'm sorry. She came at me. I didn't go after her. Please forgive me," Hollywood said as he pleaded for forgiveness.

"You wanted me to say hello for you? Well, let's call her right now. Tell her you guys are no more, and I'll let bygones be bygones."

"Are you serious?"

"Sure," Mr. Houston said as he crossed his legs.

Hollywood reached into his pocket, dialed a number, and placed the phone next to his ear. A few moments passed along. "Hey… No, I won't be able to meet up with you tonight. Or any other night. We are done." Hollywood ended the call. "See… there. It's over."

"You're right. It is over." Mr. Houston rapidly poked Hollywood in the chest with a sharp ice pick. Blood splattered on Brandon's face, but he did not flinch.

Moments later, the limo came to a complete stop. Mr. Houston placed the ice pick on the chest of Hollywood's lifeless slumped body. As he pulled off his gloves, he spat on Hollywood's forehead. Mr. Houston darted a glare at Brandon. "Don't ever bet against me again," he said, exiting the limo.

Brandon took a deep breath to process everything that had transpired. He maneuvered over to unloosen the plastic from the seats and started wrapping Hollywood's lifeless body up like a mummy.

CHAPTER 19

Justice and I sat at the bar at The Taste of Rainbow Nightclub. Justice sipped on a colorful fruity alcoholic beverage. Though there were a few people in the club, there were not as many people here as hyped and advertised. Justice flagged down a bartender.

"Would you like another one?"

"No," Justice said. "But I wanted to know where everyone was?"

"This place doesn't get rocking until ten."

I looked at my watch. "That's two hours from now. I'm not waiting around here until then. We'd have a better chance back on the Strip."

"Okay, we'll head back. I have to take a piss first." Justice rose to his feet and headed to the bathroom.

Darius, a club guest, met Justice outside of the bathroom. "Oops! I think it's one stall, but you can go first," Darius said.

"No, after you," Justice insisted.

"How about we go in together?" Darius said as he gazed into Justice's eyes.

"Nah, I'm good. I'll use the other one."

Justice entered the women's bathroom and bumped into a weeping, middle-aged-good-looking MILF who appeared to be fixing her makeup in front of the mirror. She was stoutly built like Ryan Conner back in her day. The emotional lady appeared to be fixing her makeup in front of the mirror.

"Excuse you," Jessica said.

"I'm sorry. The other one is occupied."

"Hey, it's your world. Handle your business."

Justice took a moment to capitalize on an opportunity. "I know this is weird and we're in a women's bathroom, but I think you are extremely gorgeous."

"I appreciate the compliment," said a blushing Jessica. She extended her hand. "I'm Jessica."

"I'm Justice," he said as he extended his hand.

"Pleasure meeting you, Justice."

"The pleasure is all mine. Me and my boy are about to leave. We have a suite at the Venetian. You should join us."

"I'm here with a friend."

"Oh, OK—"

"But she's cool. I'm pretty sure she wants to leave. I'll give you my number and text you when we arrive."

Justice pulled out his phone and they exchanged contact information.

CHAPTER 20

The loudness of voices, announcements, and rolling bags filled Harry Reid Airport as Brandon searched the crowd. Brandon needed to clear his mind of the brutal murder he had just witnessed, and he knew he needed to step up his attempts to develop a legitimate bankroll and get out of dodge. The degenerate gambler who betted on sports constantly hunted for an edge and his next big score. Brandon's gaze fell on a tall, young man wearing a Nevada Wolf Pack jacket who appeared lost at the baggage claim.

The young man was Jamal Thompson, one of Nevada's best players, which Brandon knew because he was a die-hard college basketball fan. Jamal was meant to be with his squad, but there were reports that his trip had been delayed due to a family emergency. This was Brandon's golden opportunity.

Brandon approached Jamal with a grin. "Jamal Thompson. Hey there, do you need a ride?"

"Yes, I missed the team bus," Jamal said. "I need to get to The Orleans for tonight's game."

"Perfect! I'm a rideshare driver," Brandon claimed, presenting a phone bearing a generic app branding. "I can take you free of charge."

Jamal paused and nodded. "That would be amazing. Thanks, man."

As they headed to the parking garage, Brandon secretly pulled out his phone and placed all of his bets on the under for Jamal's player props and the game total, betting that Jamal would not make it on time. He intended to take the "scenic" route to ensure it.

Brandon unlocked the passenger door of his beat-up vehicle and Jamal tossed his duffel bag into the backseat before hopping inside.

"Are you from Vegas?"

"Yes. Born and bred."

"You must know a lot about Vegas," Jamal said as Brandon started the car.

"Oh, you could say that," Brandon said, getting into traffic. "I've got a few of my favorite spots I could show you."

Brandon took the long route, driving through the scenic Red Rock Canyon, explaining each site with the zeal of a tour guide. "Over there is the Calico Basin. It's beautiful and great for hiking."

Jamal gazed out the window, pleased but concerned. "This is great, but I really need to be at The Orleans by six. Coach is going to bench me if I don't make the team meeting."

"Don't worry, we have plenty of time," Brandon said, comforting him, while disregarding Jamal's growing anxiousness.

To distract Jamal, Brandon kept the conversation going as they drove along the picturesque route. They spoke about basketball, life, and Brandon's manufactured tales of "rideshare" exploits. The time was ticking, and Brandon could feel Jamal's heart pounding with each passing minute. But Brandon kept his face calm.

Jamal started to become fidgety and checked his phone. "Bro! It's already five. Are we close, yet?"

"Just around the corner," Brandon said as he lied again, checking his watch. They were nowhere near The Orleans. They had spent an hour detouring down the Interstate 15, and Brandon was enjoying every second that got him closer to cashing in on his wagers.

Jamal's worry eventually reached its height. "Dude, we need to speed up. We're really cutting it close."

Brandon pretended to worry. "Oh, the traffic's terrible this time of day. Don't worry, I'll get you there as quickly as I can."

The minutes passed, and the city lights of Vegas began to glimmer as evening fell. Brandon finally headed toward The Orleans, keeping his pace moderate. Jamal's annoyance was evident, yet he remained courteous, unwilling to lash out at the man who was "helping" him.

They arrived at The Orleans around 6:30 p.m., a full half-hour beyond Jamal's scheduled arrival time. Jamal jumped out and grabbed his luggage. "Thanks, man," he said, running toward the entrance.

Brandon watched him go with a delighted grin on his face. He knew Jamal wouldn't make it in time. His wagers were practically guaranteed to win.

Brandon sped away. He had pulled it off without technically committing a crime; it was simply a "helpful" diversion that had worked out wonderfully for him. Brandon laughed as he pulled back onto the freeway.

He couldn't wait to watch the outcome of the game, knowing his under bets were safe. For Brandon, it was just another day in the life of a gambler: always searching for an advantage, always playing the game.

CHAPTER 21

Justice and I sat in the seating area of the hotel suite with two bottles of alcohol, one half filled with vodka, and the other an empty whiskey bottle.

"So, what's the plan?"

"We're going to get them drunk and not drink as much as we did last night," Justice said with conviction as he grabbed a bottle of soda and filled the empty bottle of cognac.

"How is this gonna work?"

"I'm filling the empty bottle with soda. The bottle of vodka is less than half-full but enough to get wasted. Psychologically, the ladies will choose the bottle with less alcohol."

"Are you sure?"

"Of course. I've done this a thousand times in college. I bet you it will work."

"Okay, bet it on your life."

"Now you're being ridiculous. I'm not placing a bet on my life for a piece of ass."

There was a knock at the door of the suite.

"Get the door," said Justice. "I have to finish filling the bottle."

I made my way over to greet the ladies at the door. One was a little older, but she was gorgeous. The other woman was that curly-haired rude lady from the grocery store I had confronted.

"You are a fucking asshole!" Cynthia shouted.

"You started it."

"Do you guys know each other?" Jessica asked.

"He smeared ketchup and mustard on my car."

"You cut me off, flipped me off and then ignored me when I was trying to be civil."

"Everyone chill," Justice said, mediating the situation. "Life is too short. Let's take some shots and get to know each other better."

We calmed down and walked into the sitting room area where the bottles awaited us.

"Let's play the question game. The rules are simple," Justice said. "Every time someone asks a question, you respond with a question. If you answer the question or stumble, you must take a ten-second chug from the bottle. Choices of alcohol are vodka or cognac. Ladies choose first. Pick your poison."

"I don't feel like drinking," said Cynthia.

"Come on. Play!" Jessica pleaded. "I want to feel young again. It's my birthday. It'll be like we're in our twenties again."

"You have to take another shot for your birthday," Justice insisted. Justice poured another shot of vodka for Jessica, who downed it. "Now, let the game begin. Okay, someone direct a question at me."

I leaned over and asked, "Why do questions have to be directed at you first?"

"Because it's my idea."

"You gotta drink, bitch."

Justice grabbed the bottle of what appeared to be cognac and took a big chug. The game continued.

"Do you like me?" Jessica directed her question at me.

"Can I taste you?" I directed a question to Cynthia.

"What?" Cynthia asked.

"That's not a question."

"Yes, it is. I asked 'what.'"

"Drink."

Cynthia grabbed the bottle of vodka, turned it upside down, and took a ten-second shot. Several questions and chugs later, the bottles were almost empty. The ladies appeared to be tipsier than they expected.

"Are we still playing?" Cynthia asked.

"Yep," Jessica answered.

"You gotta drink," said Cynthia.

"Oh yeah," Jessica said as she grabbed the bottle and finished it. "There is no more." She reached for the cognac.

Justice grabbed the bottle from her, and they started to kiss ferociously. They both stood to their feet.

"Let's get in the hot tub, baby!" Justice said as he guided Jessica to the bathroom.

A couple of awkward moments passed as Cynthia and I sat alone. I was not sure if I should make a move or not. Putting aside our altercation the other day, Cynthia was quite gorgeous. I moved a little closer to her. I gave Cynthia an intense sexy gaze, before going in for the kill. We started to kiss for several moments, but Cynthia pulled away.

"What are you doing?"

"I thought we were having a moment."

"I have a man. And I don't usually do stuff like this. I'm a good girl."

"What qualifies you as a good girl?"

Cynthia thought about it a second. "I go to church every Sunday—"

"Going to church doesn't make you a good girl any more than me standing in a garage and calling myself a car." I snarled at Cynthia as I studied her for a few seconds. I stood and walked over to the bathroom. I placed my ear to the door, opened it slightly, and peeked in.

"Come join us, babe."

I entered the bathroom and noticed Jessica and Justice naked in the tub.

"Take off your clothes," she said.

Moments later, one position led to another, and this lady managed to wear out both Justice and me. Justice recovered and went at her some more.

"I need a break," I said as I exited the bathroom.

"What's up?" Brandon said as he stood in the seating area of the suite.

I covered my junk with one hand and placed my arm over my nipples.

"Damn, I want your body," said Brandon, admiring my naked physique.

"Turn your damn head!"

Brandon pointed at two huge, wheeled duffel bags as he turned away. One of the bags was red and the other was black. "I got the money for the bet in each one of those bags. We each get around a hundred grand to start. I converted mine already." Brandon searched around. "Where's Justice?"

Justice walked out of the bathroom with nothing on but a towel. Brandon was slightly shocked.

"Oh no. Explain to Brandon that whatever he's thinking didn't happen."

"I don't judge."

"A woman was involved."

"You let her watch?"

"No, idiot. She was in between us. He was in the front, and I was in the back, and we swapped positions."

"Oh. Wow. Now, I see," Brandon said.

"Ironically, I met her in the bathroom at that bar you recommended. And she's a freak."

Brandon was stunningly distracted by Justice's wrist. "Is that?" Brandon approached Justice to get a better glance at Justice's flashy, diamond-studded timepiece. "Damn! It is! That's a diamond-encrusted Patek Philipp! I've always wanted one. Man, I bet you could buy a car with the money you spent on that thing!"

"You already know!" Justice said, trying to suppress a blush.

Brandon grabbed Justice's wrist to study the watch. "Oh, my goodness, it's even more breathtaking in person! Look at those diamonds sparkle! Can I have it?"

"Yeah... OK... never," Justice said with a chuckle.

Jessica walked out of the bathroom with her hair all over her head. "That was so much fun."

Brandon's irritation ignited as his focus was no longer fixated on Justice's wristwatch. "Jessie!" Brandon shouted with disgust.

"Jessie? Wait! She said her name was Jessica. Jessie is a guy's name. Which means...oh god! Don't tell me she's—"

"My mother," Brandon confirmed.

Wait! What? Mother!? I cannot believe this is Brandon's mother. Justice and I never met Brandon's biological mother growing up, so to meet her like this is outlandish, to say the least. I cannot believe this is somebody's momma. Wow! I thought he was about to say she was a man. There was an awkward pause in the room. Jessica scurried over to the seating area, grabbed her purse, kissed Brandon on the cheek, and exited the suite.

We three stood with our own twisted, complex thoughts. My first thought was that maybe if I stood real still, Brandon would forget I was in the room. My second thought was that I was not sure if I should laugh or make a joke about it. He would not like jokes I had about her lips on his face, especially after knowing where she had put them a few moments before.

"I'm gonna go find some clothes," I said as I reentered the bathroom, locking the door, so that Justice had been left behind for Brandon to confront. At that moment, this was a future family affair.

CHAPTER 22

Jessica tiptoed through the dark-lit bedroom. She stripped off her clothes and attempted to sneak into bed but the noise of a pumping shotgun froze Jessica. The light turned on. Mr. Houston was in bed in his pajamas holding a sawed-off Mossberg shotgun.

"It's just me, baby," said Jessica.

Mr. Houston slowly lowered the shotgun to the side of the bed. "Why are you in my house?" he asked firmly.

"This is my house too, Dallas."

"Oh, is that so? Name one bill that you've paid?"

Jessica was taken aback. "I…well…you make more money than me."

"What meals do you prepare for me daily?"

"But, Dallas, we have a chef."

"Yes, there is a chef that I pay for. Do you even clean up your messes?"

"I try to, but the cleaning ladies get to my mess before I get a chance to clean it up."

"Yes! And I also pay for the cleaning ladies. You don't cook nor do you clean. You run that shithole club that costs me money. Running around in the streets like some Gen Z-er. You're nothing to me but a lying, cheating liability."

"I don't get it, Dallas," a frustrated Jessica said. "We loved each other once before. You used to treat me like your queen. You said I was the only woman for you. Now you treat me like a slut."

"That's because you gave me chlamydia."

Jessica is taken aback yet again. "That was a month ago, Dallas. Why are we still living in the past?"

Dallas walked up to Jessica and started to sniff her as if he were a curious dog. "You smell like sex."

"I smell like sex for you, baby," Jessica said as she seductively rubbed against Mr. Houston.

Mr. Houston smacked Jessica's face, grabbed her by the throat and stared deep into her eyes as she gasped for air. "Go shower."

Jessica caught her breath as she gathered herself and headed for the shower. Mr. Houston got back in bed and snuggled up with his shotgun.

CHAPTER 23

A flustered yet angered Brandon paced the floor for obvious reasons. "You guys don't know what you've done."

"This was an honest mistake. We never met your mother growing up," Justice said. "Besides, you and Emily have different mothers."

"Right," I said, chiming in. "But the irony is you that said you would bang my mother and yours was the one that got banged."

Brandon charged forward, but Justice held him back.

"Let him go," I said.

"Fuck you, Terrence. You motherfucker."

"I mean, I am a motherfucker."

"You wanna go right now!" Brandon said, squaring up as if he was ready to fight. "Fuck you!" Brandon shouted at me.

"Fuck you back," I responded.

"I said it first," Brandon said as he stuck his tongue out at me.

"Can we stop reacting like little boys here? We're men right," Justice said.

"He started it," Brandon said with a pout as he pointed at me then crossed his arms.

"No! You started it when you said you would smash my mother. But Justice and I finished."

Brandon charged forward at me again. Justice got in between us again.

"You're not helping the situation, Terrence."

"Get your hands off of me," Brandon roared as he pushed Justice off of him.

"I'm the victim here," I said. "It is both of y'all's fault this happened. Brandon recommended going to the damn club. Justice met up with your mother there, and they invited me in the hot tub with them."

"It wasn't out of malice, bro," Justice said with deep compassion. "We didn't know that was your mom."

"You know what? Fine! But I'm taking my bills back," Brandon said as he grabbed the handle of the bags filled with bills and dragged them near the door.

"You take those bills out of this room and I'm big-time snitching," I said as I walked over to the room's phone.

A livid Brandon took a deep breath. "My mom owns that bar. I didn't think you guys would end up meeting and sleeping with her."

"If my research is correct, Dallas Houston owns that club," Justice said.

"Yep! He's the guy that married my mom and took her away from me."

"Wow! We banged my boss's wife."

"Don't brag about that in public. Dallas is an extremely jealous man. He's dangerous," Brandon said coldly.

"Mr. Houston?" Justice inquired with a chuckle.

Brandon nodded. "I'm serious. Do not tell anyone that you slept with that man's wife. You have to lay low and let me figure this out."

"Figure out what?" Justice asked with concern.

At first, it was fun getting revenge on Brandon for those snide comments he made about my mother. But as I studied Brandon's face and body language, it felt like there was something a bit more complex than him being mad at friends for banging his mother.

"Is it cool if I can get my cut?" Justice said as he stared at his phone. "I have somewhere to be."

"I was thinking we play a game of Monopoly to split the profits."

Justice and I both stared at each other.

"Whoever wins gets the majority share of the bills, and the other two players share a third of the pot," Brandon said, pulling out a gameboard of Monopoly.

This Monopoly was the updated version of the game. All of the original locations on the board were the same. Some of the tokens were the same, but the boot, wheelbarrow, or thimble pieces were missing. Those tokens were replaced with a T-Rex, a rubber ducky, and a penguin.

I picked up the three new tokens. "Uh, bro, when's the last time you saw a T-Rex or a penguin?"

"If you have a problem with my board, buy your own," Brandon said with a bit of sass.

A nervous Justice scanned the room as he looked down at his watch. "Nah, I'm good," Justice said.

"You're scared Terrence might beat your ass again," Brandon said.

I tried to conceal the smile on my face because I knew Justice did not want any smoke.

"I'm not scared. I don't have time. Let's just efficiently split the money up in three ways."

"Whoever holds the gold makes the rules," Brandon said.

The room grew quiet as tension slid into it. You could cut the tension in the room with a rubber knife.

"Whatever," said Justice. "Let's do it."

The functionality of the game remained the same. The significant difference was the credit cards that took the place of the Monopoly bills and the pacing of the play. There was an electronic banking system device that added, subtracted, and exchanged money for each other's cards. The electronic banker unit prevented players from stealing money from the bank. Instead of starting with $1,500, each player started with 1.5 million dollars. And every time you passed go, you got 250 thousand dollars.

To start the game off properly, the banker, which was Brandon, shuffled the title deed cards and dealt them out to Justice and me. We, as players, must immediately pay the banker the price of the properties we received. You only needed to build three houses instead of four on each side of the color group before buying a hotel. When selling hotels, the value was half its purchase price. As soon as the first player went bankrupt, the game ended, and the banker used the banker unit to add up the money. The richest player won the game.

The game commenced. It was just a matter of time until one of these fools landed on my property and went bankrupt. The fun part was the middle, where we considered probabilities and board positions. Justice made deals with Brandon but ignored me at all costs. It was here where skill won or lost the game.

An hour had passed since the start of the game.

I was the battleship game-piece. I will always be the battleship piece because I have a battleship personality in real life. I could float by you peacefully or blow your shit up if the situation required. My ship was currently docked on Pennsylvania Railroad. I owned all the red and green properties, and there were hotels on all of them. I was sitting on 25 million on my bank card.

Justice was the racing car game-piece because he's pretentious and into flashy stuff. He had 15 million dollars on his card and owned Boardwalk, Park Place, and some orange properties with hotels on them. His car was parked on the Chance space.

Brandon, who chased his tail and humped many legs for much of his life, held the dog token. Dogs are about as intelligent as a two-year-old, and that is where I think Brandon's intellect lies at times.

Brandon owned the light blue and magenta properties with many homes but no hotels and less than a million dollars on his card. It was Brandon's turn to roll the dice after two consecutive doubles landed him on FREE PARKING. Brandon rolled the dice. It was a double two. Brandon moved his piece to jail. "I would rather go to jail," he said.

Justice grabbed the dice, then rolled a ten. He hesitated to move his game piece because his next move landed him on North Carolina Avenue, which was my property that had a hotel on it. A shit-eating grin flashed across my face.

"How much do I owe?" Justice said, avoiding eye contact with me.

I examined the back of the deed card. "That will be 12,750,000 of them thangs."

Justice snatched the card from my hand and studied the back of the card. He frowned and tossed the card back at me. "Whatever," he said, handing Brandon his credit card.

"It's not fun when the rabbit has the gun," I said, antagonizing Justice. He was a different person whenever he was not winning. How you act when you lose lets me know how you are whenever you win.

Brandon showed me my new balance, and my card now had $38 million in the account. I wished I had this much money in my real account.

It was my turn to roll. I grabbed the dice and rolled a four, which landed me on New York Avenue. Fortunately for me, it was Brandon's property, and he only had two homes on it.

It was Brandon's turn to roll the dice. He rolled a three. He either had to pay to get out of jail or roll a double. "Welp, I guess I'll stay in jail."

Justice grabbed the dice, shook them up in his hand a little longer, blew on them, then rolled. Snake eyes. That only moved him two spots and placed Justice's car on Pennsylvania Avenue, which I own. It cost 14 million dollars. I grew smug, realizing I had bankrupted Justice, and the game was over.

Justice scanned me up and down but said nothing. Anger, disappointment, frustration, and envy were written all over his face. Justice shoulder-checked me as he stormed toward the door.

"Now, all we got to do is transmute the fake bills into bigger bills," Brandon said.

"Oh, lord," I said. "Any time someone starts a sentence with 'all-we-got-to-do-is' usually means one of us is going to jail."

"I'm not wasting a free weekend of debauchery on your little scam," Justice professed. "I'll probably win the bet without your little fake bills. Terrence, you can have my stash. Just make sure when I win you guys pay me in real currency." Justice's phone rang. "Hello… Hey…OK. I'm on my way." He hung up the phone. Justice glanced at his watch. "I have somewhere to be, but just a heads up, we were invited to a housewarming party. It is at one of my client's houses. I'm guessing women will be there."

"If there will be free food and women? Count me in." The excited Brandon placed his arm around me.

I shoved Brandon's arm off.

"I'll text you the address. His name is Victor Michaels. I think you guys used to work together or something."

"Victor Michaels? That is Shontae's new boyfriend."

"Oh, shit, that's right," Justice said with a chuckle. "I didn't think about that."

"Bro, why would you be cool with a guy like Victor?" I asked.

"Chill, Terrence. I'm cool with everybody."

I crossed my arms. "If you're cool with everybody, you ain't loyal to anybody."

"Whatever! You don't have to go. You can sit here and pout about it for all I care."

"At least I'm not crying about it in a club like you were the other night."

"That was a sensitive subject," Justice said as he hustled out of the suite, mumbling, "Terrence's always bringing up old shit."

Brandon rolled me one of the bags. "Well, these bills won't convert themselves," he said as he exited the suite, and I followed right behind.

CHAPTER 24

We made our way onto the casino floor and walked toward the cashier's cage. The duffel bag I was carrying was heavier than it looked. It felt as if I was rolling around with a midsized human in the bag. We reached the cage with a long line of guests waiting to cash in their gambling chips.

I stuck my hand in the bag to feel the texture of the $1 bills. There were multiple stacks of rubber-banded bills.

"We have to convert the bills someplace where we can catch them slipping," Brandon said. "A place that doesn't use a counterfeit bill detection machine."

We both stood and thought about it for several moments.

"Are you thinking what I'm thinking?"

I nodded yes. But my mouth said, "No."

"Strippers. They deal with singles all day, every day. Let's go to a strip club, talk with the strippers, and see if they could help us exchange our dollars."

"I guess," I said unenthused.

"What do you have against strippers?"

"I don't like the male-to-female ratio with strippers."

"Male-to-female ratio?"

"Yes. Think of all the men that a stripper comes in contact with daily. And I am sure there are a shit ton of men just like you that don't wash their hands. Think about how many guys have placed their faces or hands on a stripper's chest. Those boobs are contaminated, and they wanna stick them in my face? I just don't want a stripper sitting on my lap after they've sat on thirty different guys' laps. It's unsanitary."

"We're going there for business."

"Yes, strictly business."

Brandon dug into his pocket, grabbed his phone, and went through the messages. "The driver will be here in a few. I have to take this call." Brandon walked a few feet away but close enough for me to overhear bits of the conversation. "Hey, sis…OK…Yeah…What? That's crazy… Okay…I'll contact her." Brandon walked back over. "You mind if I meet you at the strip club? I have a quick errand."

"Don't make me go there by myself," I pleaded.

"It will only be for a few minutes," Brandon said. He dug into his purse and pulled out a thick knot of $100 bills. He fingered through them, then handed them to me. "These are not fake, by the way. Entertain yourself until I get there."

I stuffed the bills in my pocket.

Brandon leaned in and whispered, "If you need to convert some singles, use the red bag. The bills in the black bag are vacuumed and sealed." Brandon glanced down at his phone. "The driver is pulling up, soon. It's a silver Prius."

Brandon took off in the other direction, and I headed to the rideshare area.

CHAPTER 25

Justice was in a nice, cozy neighborhood not too far from the Las Vegas Strip called Spring Valley. Clothes were scattered across the apartment and led into the bathroom where Karla and Justice were cuddled up in a hot tub next to a half bottle of red wine. Justice's phone started to vibrate.

"What's the origin behind your name?" Karla asked.

"My mother. She named me after the movie *Poetic Justice*."

"Oh, I loved that film," Karla said. She stared into Justice's eyes. "Can I be honest?"

"Sure."

"I know you're engaged, but I think I'm really into what we have been building together. I have been on a few dates with guys that I have met online but nobody quite like you. But I totally understand that you will be married soon."

Justice took a couple of moments to soak in Karla's words. "Reflecting on everything. I don't think I will be marrying my fiancée anymore. I thought I wanted to be single. But I don't want to be single. I want to be with you."

Karla grabbed Justice's head, and they started kissing. Justice's phone rang again. Simultaneously, the doorbell began to ring. After stopping momentarily, it rang once again. And again. They continued to kiss.

"Give me a second," Karla said as she got out of the tub, grabbed her robe, and rushed off. Karla walked through the living room and opened the door to see Mr. Houston.

"What are you doing here?"

"Can we talk?" he asked.

"There is nothing for us to talk about, Dallas," Karla said as she attempted to slam the door, but Mr. Houston stopped the door with his shoe.

"Don't you dare," Mr. Houston said with a growl. "I'm not here for that. I'm here about the documents. Did you make those edits to my accounts like I asked you to?"

"I'm not doing it. I could go to jail for falsifying federal tax files."

"It's a slim possibility, Karla. All that needs to be done by you is to take the old figures and switch them with the new figures," Mr. Houston said, handing her a binder.

"I can't do it. That is how I lost my last job. I can't risk it at my job and I'm not going to jail for you."

"But what about the things I bought you?"

"I thought that was because you and I were—"

"You thought I was paying to have sex with you? I have a wife whom I overpay to sleep with. This was business, sweetheart. You wanted things, and I provided them. Now you have to do something for me."

A toilet flushed in the background. Mr. Houston took a second to let the moment process.

"If I go down, so will you. Because they'll take everything my name is on. Your car, your home, and your parents' home. Everything will be gone," Mr. Houston said and then stormed off.

Moments later, Karla returned to the bathroom.

"What's that about?"

"Nothing," she said as she tossed the binder in the trash bin.

Justice hopped out of the tub and dried off. He reached for his clothes. "I have to get to work. My boss called several times."

"Okay. Well, there's one more thing before you go." Karla said as her robe dropped to the floor. She walked toward Justice and started to kiss and suck on his neck.

"I don't know if I have enough energy for a fifth round, baby," Justice said. Although the words out of his mouth said the opposite, he lifted her off of her feet and they started to make out ferociously.

CHAPTER 26

Brandon sat in the chair, twiddling his thumbs. Agent Thurman entered the room and took a seat across from Brandon.

"I'm Agent Leslie Thurman of the FBI. We have reasons to believe that you're making counterfeit bills, or someone is supplying you with them."

"I don't know what you're talking about, but I posted bail thirty minutes ago."

"You didn't think anybody was gonna find out?"

"Find out what? I came here to file a restraining order, and the police arrested me."

"That is because *you* had warrants. Let's talk about what we found in your wallet."

Brandon became a little nervous. "I don't have a clue what you're talking about."

"Counterfeit bills."

"I don't know anything about counterfeit bills. All the cash I had was given to me as an allowance."

"An allowance? From whom?

"My stepfather."

"Who is?"

"Dallas Houston."

The agent wrote the name down.

"I'll gladly testify if need be but…uh…Agent Thurman, I posted bail already. I should be free to go, right?"

"You're free to go for now."

Brandon stood and walked off.

"We'll be in touch again soon," Thurman proclaimed.

CHAPTER 27

I sat in a secluded corner away from the stage of The Velvet Room. I made sure to sit far away from the thirsty men throwing dollars at the dancers on stage because I did not want any attention on me. People watched as I rolled the duffel bags of cash next to me. This place reeked of desperation as men threw money at dancers on the stage. I will say this: the most physically gifted and masterfully shaped woman you will ever see is at a strip club. If you live in Las Vegas, you most certainly have seen a dancer from the strip club working out at your local Las Vegas Athletic Club.

Some of the strippers had fake asses. Most people could spot a BBL from a mile away because of the thigh-to-ass ratio. You could also spot a fake ass by where it sat. If a butt sat too high and poked out like a disfigured watermelon; that there is a fake ass. That is no knock on the phony-ass-getters, but there is nothing like a natural one. The kind of bottom you know she got from her mama.

"Hey, sweetheart," a stripper said as she approached, then sat on my lap.

"Go get your money, baby. I'm not donating today."

"Whatever," she said with a bit of sass as she jumped off. She found another guy's lap to sit on, and I was chopped liver.

I glanced at my phone and noticed an hour had passed since I'd last seen Brandon.

A cocktail waitress approached. "Would you like something to drink?"

"I'm good. Thank you," I said as I observed the ambiance. "Who owns this place?"

"Lorenzo Carlucci."

I nodded as I dug in my pocket and counted the bills Brandon handed me. I counted thirty-six bills, which equated to $3,600, and placed most of the bills in my pocket except for three $100 bills. I handed her one of the bills.

"Thank you. Let me know if there is anything else you need," she said and walked off.

As I scanned the room, another stripper aimed toward my lap.

"Please don't sit on me."

She instead sat in a chair next to me.

"Why are you sitting here by yourself?"

"Just life," I said, to keep it short.

"So, life brought you here to be aloof?"

"Aloof?" I questioned. "That's a pretty big word for a stripper."

"It's not a big word. It only has five letters."

"Oh, she so smart, I see. Let me guess, you're a college student and you do this part-time?"

"Graduated already and I work full-time."

"So, you're a college graduate, but you're still dancing full-time?"

"I still have to pay for that damn degree," she said with a chuckle.

My curiosity had been struck. "What was your major?"

"Bachelor of Science in Business Administration and Real Estate."

"Respect. I'm Terrence, by the way," I said, extending my hand.

She chuckled but accepted my greeting. "It's Denice."

"Denice?! That's a clever stripper name said no one ever," I said teasing. "Did you come up with that all by yourself?"

"No. My mother helped. It's my real name, Terrence."

"Oh, I feel so special. Denice gave me her real name."

"I'm surprised you don't recognize me. We used to work together at the insurance company."

I took a closer glimpse at her in the dark-lit club and realized who she was. "Denice!? Dorky Denice with the nice—"

Denice stood and turned around.

"Wow!" I was lost for words. She was completely unrecognizable until she stood up. "I did not know you were stripping. Do you like it?"

"I mean, it has its perks. There have been times I've been given loads of cash just to converse. It's sort of like being a naked licensed therapist. Except we don't get paid like a licensed therapist. The money is good some days. Sometimes, it is stressful to leave work owing more than I've earned to cover tip-out and house fees. But some customers appreciate and empathize with the struggle."

"Doesn't that get old, though? How does that make you feel about getting objectified for a paycheck?"

"Have you not lived in America? Objectification is big business. There are so many women making money off of Instagram and OnlyFans. You guys stared at me for free when we all worked together. Why not make money from it if it will happen regardless?"

"How did you get in the business?"

It took her a moment to gather her thoughts. "My mother died in a car wreck when I was a senior in high school. I didn't want my little sister to go into foster care or go to my asshole of a father, so I started dancing while attending college."

"How much do you owe?"

"About twenty-five grand."

"What's the max you've made in a night?"

"Why? Are you trying to match it?"

"Maybe."

"There are days I've made as much as fifteen hundred and as little as three dollars."

I scanned the room to make sure the coast was clear. I leaned in so she would be the only one that could hear what I was about to say. "I need to convert some singles into bigger bills, but I don't want to make a scene. If I give you twenty grand in singles, do you think you can bring back fifteen grand in big bills?" I unzipped the red bag a little so she could peek in.

Denice peeked into it and her eyes lit up. "What's the catch?"

"No catch. I give you twenty grand, and you convert that into big bills for me. You'll earn $3,500 more than your biggest payout."

She thought about it. "Okay, give it to me."

I opened the bag a little more, and her eyes grew big. I handed her a few stacks of bills.

"I'm not sure we can exchange all of these at this club."

"Let's just focus on the bills I gave you."

"Okay," she said walking away with the stacks of bills I handed her.

Several moments later, she returned and handed me two small stacks, one for $10,000 and the other for $5,000.

Brandon made his way over to where we were sitting.

"I've converted some of the bills already. I think we can convert the others if we talk to the owner."

"The owner might have a problem with it," said Brandon.

"How do you know?"

"Trust me," Brandon said convincingly. "How much did you convert?"

"I paid her five grand to bring back fifteen racks."

"Let's get rid of the bills in the red bag. What's your friend's name?"

"Denice."

"Denice, can you bring over three or four of your girls? Tell them the same deal is on the table Terrence offered you."

Denice walked away.

"The feds are on to me, so we have to spread the bills out fast so that it doesn't trace back to us. The more people involved, the better we can spread the confusion."

Denice returned with four other dancers. One of them was the stripper that had sat on my lap earlier.

"Everyone except for her can stay." The stripper flipped me off and walked away. Brandon and I started handing out stack after stack of $1 bills until the red bag was empty. In a matter of hours, we were up $75,000 cash. It was not a bad night for the dancers either. Denice made ten grand, and the other three dancers made five grand apiece.

Brandon passed out several $100 bills to each of the dancers. "You didn't see us. If anyone asked where the bills came from, tell them it came from Dallas Houston." All of the dancers veered off into their perspective corners except for Denice.

"What's the deal with the black bag?" I asked Brandon.

"I have special plans for this one," Brandon said, gripping the handle of the black duffel bag. "We'll need a car, though."

"Okay, we'll take mine."

"Cool. Let's get out of here." Brandon rolled the bag toward the entrance.

Denice gave me a big hug. "Thank you, Terrence."

"Stay in touch."

"I will."

Before I exited the strip club, I took one last glance at the gorgeous dancer named Denice. She waved. I waved back. I might have fallen in love with a stripper, but just like that, the feelings faded as a guy walked up and whispered something in her ear. She grabbed his hand and guided him toward the VIP room. I followed behind after Brandon. We had bigger things on the horizon.

CHAPTER 28

Justice drove up to a beautiful apartment complex near Summerlin and parked his new Chevrolet Corvette in a vacant handicap spot in the semi-vacant parking lot. He sat with his thoughts a few moments before reaching for his phone. Justice scrolled through his phone and found some seductive photos Karla had sent him days ago. She was everything Justice wanted because she matched his sex drive. But he also thought about the life decisions he already made with Emily. Justice knew he needed to decide soon whether it was the right one or not.

Justice stepped out of his car and rushed to the back of the vehicle's trunk. The back of his car was filled with boxes and bags of women's clothing. Justice grabbed two large plastic storage containers and threw a trash bag full of articles on top, closed the trunk, and walked toward the lobby entrance of the apartment building. He continued to walk through the building.

Justice stuck his key in the door. He entered the vacant residence, placed the boxes and bags in the middle of the space on the floor, and headed for the door. Before exiting, he took out the thumb drive Mr. Houston left on his desk and placed it on top of the pile of things.

Justice scrolled through his phone as he walked toward the parking lot. He typed out a text to Emily: *I know this is cowardly of me, but I feel like I have allowed the opinions of others to influence the decisions I have made involving us. And I will now be taking back my life. I will be there for our future child, but I do not want to be the future husband that you need. I understand that your lease is up and I knew that you had intentions of us moving in together, so I went ahead and leased a place for you in Summerlin near your mother. The first year is paid in full. All you need to gain access to the apartment is to contact the property managers and they will provide you with the key. I'm sorry it had to be this way. I know you'll feel this isn't fair to you but it is also not fair to me. I will be here if you need me but not as a lover.*

Justice took a deep breath right before he sent the message. He muted any future calls and messages that Emily would send to avoid her emotional reaction to his latest decision.

As Justice made his way out of the apartment building, an all-black limo pulled in front of him nearly striking him. "Mr. Houston," Justice said nervously as he looked around with concern. "What brings you to this area?"

"I own this property," Mr. Houston said before he kicked open the car door. "Hop in. It'll only be a few moments."

Justice and Mr. Houston sat quietly in the backseat of the limo. The windows were tinted dark, and the seats were covered in black plastic bags.

Mr. Houston sat aloof as he stared out of the window before slowly bringing his attention to Justice. "Idiots believe in that 'American Dream' bullshit. They take out loans to buy cars, homes, boats, jewelry, vacations, things that make them poor. I take out loans to buy land and buildings that make me rich," Mr. Houston said as he stared at Justice. "Hiring you has been very profitable for my bottom line, but now we've met at a fork in the road."

"I'm not sure I'm following, sir."

"Justice, you were an outstanding student. You're the only one that listened to me. You have been working for me for six years. Do you know how much money I've made off of you?"

"A few million."

"Roughly twenty-six million to be exact," Mr. Houston said. "My question to you is: can you afford her?"

"Uh…sir!"

"I pay you a handsome salary at my company. I know how much you make. It's not how much you make; it's how much you keep and how many generations you keep it for. But can you afford to keep her?" Mr. Houston said as he put on rubber gloves.

Terror struck Justice. "Mr. Houston, I can explain."

"Where did you go to college again?"

"Stanford," a nervous Justice said.

"Stanford, that's right. Believe it or not, Justice, I dropped out of college. I earned a PhD from the streets. The idea of wasting years learning something I'll never use and paying for a piece of paper to justify my intelligence never intrigued me. 'A' students work for 'C' students."

Mr. Houston brought out a pistol.

"It was an accident. We didn't know who she was?"

Mr. Houston's face contorted. "We?" he questioned. "Who the fuck is we?"

"My roommate and I…we slept with your wife."

The tension in Mr. Houston's face grew tighter. He threw an envelope on Justice's lap. Justice opened the envelope, revealing three photos of Justice and Karla hanging out together on different occasions. One of the photos was a recent photo of Justice and Karla kissing outside of the Allure Lounge a few nights ago.

"If I understand this correctly," Mr. Houston said as he cogitated a bit on his next words. "You and another guy slept with my wife. And you're currently sleeping with my Karla," he said as he brought the barrel of the gun to Justice's temple. Suddenly, a white van pulled behind the limo.

"The guys are here, boss," Mr. Houston's driver said.

Mr. Houston lowered the pistol. "Can you place your hand on the center console?"

Justice placed his hand where he was told. Mr. Houston set the gun down next to Justice practically daring him to take the pistol. Mr. Houston pulled out a small hammer and smashed it against Justice's hand.

Justice screeched in agony from the hammer blow.

"This is a warning. Stay away from Karla. Now, get the fuck out of my car."

Justice nursed his wounded hand as he exited the car.

"Oh, and about that promotion, we do not require your services anymore."

The vehicle sped off, leaving Justice in pain and baffled.

CHAPTER 29

Mr. Houston rode along in the back seat of the car. His phone rang. He scanned the number before answering the call. It was Reverend Hillman.

"A couple of people missed payments, including Charles," Reverend Hillman said through the phone. "I found out he was sent to jail. He hasn't paid his dues in almost twenty-four months. I sent the guys over to collect, but no one answered."

"If he doesn't pay by tomorrow morning, send the guys back over and tell them to put their hands on his wife if she does not cooperate."

"Excuse me?

"You heard me. Tell those knuckleheads to torture her but do not kill her just yet." He ended the call and gazed out of the window as the car road along the streets.

CHAPTER 30

Brandon and I parked several feet away from the megachurch, Planet Changers House parking lot. The church, with about 20,000 members, was in North Las Vegas.

Reverend Hillman was about a few hundred feet away from where we were parked. He paced back and forth and appeared to be engaged in a heated conversation over the phone.

"Can you believe this clown? Reverend Hillman set up a GoFundMe campaign to pay for a three-million-dollar yacht. What the hell kind of worship services require you to purchase a yacht? And I'm not good enough for his daughter."

"That's right. I forgot that was Shontae's father. You know he does business with my shady-ass stepfather, Dallas. It's like hundreds of thousands of dirty untaxed cash that is flushed through the church weekly. They use the church to launder most of the town's money. Did you know the average amount given per member is $17 a week? That's around $74 a month and $884 a year per tither. Times that by twenty-something-thousand members and divide that by fifty-two."

"That's over a million dollars in donations plus the national TV rights," I said.

"Yep! Remember that mortuary I got fired from? Reverend Hillman also owned it. I was one of the drivers of those white vans parked up front. Those things transferred corpses along with money. I know the ins and outs of their whole operation. Another white van should be pulling up right about..." Brandon looked at his watch and the white van pulled in and parked behind the already parked white van in front of the church.

Brandon hopped in the backseat of the vehicle. He pulled out a tan money bag, unzipped the black duffel bag, took out the vacuum-sealed bricks of $1 bills, and stuffed them in a tan bag.

"I don't know about this, bro," I said, becoming a tad bit apprehensive. "I feel like we're robbing God."

"We're not robbing God. We're robbing a church that uses God to make money."

He was right. God does not need anyone's money. Still trying to convince myself this plan was solid, I asked, "Are you sure this is gonna work?"

"Not really," said a slightly confident Brandon. "But we're about to fuck around and find out."

The men got out of the van and greeted Reverend Hillman.

"I have a confession," Brandon said. "Remember those girls we linked up with a couple of days ago?" Brandon asks.

"Yeah, what about them?"

"We kinda worked together until they stole my wallet. They are escorts but without the sex part. One chick does the seducing. The other girl picks the pockets and takes the money. And I come in to save them from having to have sex with dudes. Most are married men, so I take a few photos and use it as blackmail material. People pay good money to hide their secrets here in Vegas. We all three typically split the profits. But guess who popped up one day?"

"Hillman?"

Brandon nodded yes.

"No fucking way."

"Yes, fucking way. I still have the pictures. I'll send them over to you and do with them as you like."

The homeless man hid in the bushes several feet away from the van and the men working for the church.

Brandon signaled for the bum to come over to the car. The homeless man approached the passenger-side window. "Remember, this is just like opening kickoff back in the day," Brandon said as he made a rumbling sound that mimicked a loud kickoff roar.

The bum revved up and charged forward like a bull. Seconds later. *SMACK!* The homeless man speared a guy carrying a tan bag that matched the bag Brandon filled. The bag was loose like a wet football. The bum scrambled around to take possession of the bag. He recovered the bag, then darted off as if heading for the end-zone to score a touchdown. The workers in the white van chased after the bum, but they could not keep up.

The bum hauled ass several blocks until I pulled in front of him and cut him off. The bum rolled over the hood of my car and landed hard on the pavement. Brandon hopped out of the car and grabbed the tan bag next to the bum, who was unconscious. He switched the tan bag out with the one in the backseat.

"Get out of here!" Brandon said as he waved me away.

"What about him?"

"He's good," Brandon said. "I made sure he was high as hell so he wouldn't feel a thing."

I jumped in the car and sped off.

Brandon hustled back to the church and returned the tan bag to Reverend Hillman.

"Thank you, young man," Reverend Hillman said, extending his greetings.

Brandon instead went in for a hug. "The pleasure is all mine," said Brandon. He kissed the reverend on the cheek, then dashed off.

"We gotta go," one of the drivers of the white van said. "We have to get this over to Mr. Houston. He's already at the bank waiting for us."

The drivers finished loading the vans, shut all of the doors, and drove off one by one.

~

Several moments later, Brandon and I linked back up a few blocks away in a random parking lot. We turned the tan bag upside down and dumped stacks of $100 bills, $50 bills, and $20 bills. The beauty of it all was that they were authentic bills.

"Are you kidding me?" I said emphatically. "How did you think of this?"

"I stole the idea from one of the guys I used to work with."

"If you don't split this cash with me, I'm snitching, bro."

"Relax, I'm splitting it," Brandon said.

I looked to the back seat where there was still a massive pile of loose fake bills. "What about the rest of the fake ones?"

Brandon thought about it for a second. "I got an idea what we could do with them."

CHAPTER 31

A long line of patient patrons awaited their turn to speak with a bank teller. Mr. Houston appeared frustrated as he sat in the lobby. He got to his feet, walked to the front of the line, and asked the teller, "What's the holdup, Ma'am?"

"I apologize for the inconvenience, Mr. Houston," the teller said.

"It's never inconveniently taken seventeen minutes and thirteen seconds to deposit cash."

"Yes, sir! But there appears to be a problem with some of the bills."

"What do you mean?"

"Dallas Houston," Special Agent Thurman said as she flashed her badge.

Mr. Houston turned around to see federal agents surrounding him.

"You have the right to remain silent," said Agent Thurman. "Anything you say will be used against you in court; you have the right to consult with an attorney and to have that attorney present during questioning."

One of the agents placed handcuffs on Mr. Houston and escorted him out of the bank. Mr. Houston was loaded into an unmarked vehicle.

From there, Mr. Houston was transported into custody, where he was photographed, fingerprinted, and placed into an interrogation room for questioning.

Mr. Houston and Agent Thurman sat at the table across from each other in the interrogation room. The agent pulled out a stack of $1 bills and tossed it to Mr. Houston.

"These are the counterfeit bills you've created and have been blanketing around town. We also confiscated some from your stepson Brandon Perez, who said he got them from you."

Mr. Houston began to chuckle.

"What do you find funny, Mr. Houston?"

"Brandon is a con artist! He set me up."

"Everything traces back to you. Furthermore, your last deposit was a significant amount of fake one-dollar bills."

"You can't charge me with counterfeiting. I am a businessman who generates real capital."

"Probably not. But what we did charge you with was embezzlement, bank fraud, and false bank statements that you have submitted over the last several years. We also have secured testimony against you from a close associate."

Mr. Houston grew cold for a few seconds. He took a deep breath and gathered his composure. "I'd like to see my lawyer, now."

CHAPTER 32

We made it back to the sketchy location in downtown Las Vegas, the lowest and dirtiest part of the city, SKID ROW. It was an area of cheap hotels, pawnshops, secondhand stores, and missions that cater to the homeless. The sidewalks were lined with cardboard boxes, tents, and shopping carts.

I crept through the neighborhood slowly as Brandon stuck his head out of the sunroof and began to dump $1 bills into the middle of the street.

A bum ran over, picked a few bills off the ground, and studied them. "Hey, guys," she yelled ecstatically. "It's money!"

A few bills floated over and hit another homeless person in the face, awakening him from his three-day nap. A few other homeless people ran to the middle of the street and examined the bills.

All of a sudden, a chaotic bum war erupted, shopping carts, cardboard boxes, and feces flying all over the place.

We watched from afar as they fought against each other. It was fascinating to watch until the battle stopped. They all turned and started to gravitate to the source of where the money came from: my car.

Brandon bounced back in the car. "Uh…Terrence! Drive!"

I took a glimpse at the rearview mirror and noticed the herd of bums attacking the car like zombies.

Brandon screamed, "Oh my God! Oh my God! Oh my God!"

"Shut up!" I yelled as I sped off.

Brandon attempted to calm himself down as he caught his breath. "I have a better idea."

~

A few blocks later, we were at another strip club. We sat at the base of the stage at another gentlemen's club. We balled up $1 bills and tossed them at the dancer as if she were a basketball goal, the dancer providing a hoop for us with her legs as she did a headstand.

Brandon started to make it rain, but it got on me. I turned and gave Brandon a stern stare. He stopped.

My phone vibrated in my pocket. A message from Justice. The message read; *I have to stop by the emergency room then heading to Victor's spot for the housewarming. Here's the address in case you guys want to pull up. 1111 Willow Ridge Lane, Southern Highlands, NV.*

Emergency room? What happened? I texted.

Justice texted back; *Shit got real. Too much to text. Hand is throbbing.*

Brandon's phone rang. He answered it and placed the call on speaker, "Talk to me."

~

On the other side of town was the bum from earlier hiding in the bushes a few feet away from Mr. Houston's limo. "He's here, boss! He's here!" the homeless man said.

Moments later, Mr. Houston burst through the doors of Reverend Hillman's office.

"Everything okay?" the preacher asked.

Mr. Houston drew a pistol down on Reverend Hillman. Reverend Hillman reached for the sky.

"I was arrested today because of counterfeit bills," said Mr. Houston.

"Counterfeit bills?" Reverend Hillman questioned. "Where did they come from?"

"The bills came from the Sunday's deposit."

"I run a clean operation here. I had nothing to do with that. My reputation is on the line. I can't afford that kind of negativity," the reverend began to say before he was interrupted by a random phone ringing in the room.

"I thought I told you no phones," Mr. Houston said.

"It's not my phone," the reverend said as he searched around. He discovered a phone vibrating in his coat pocket. He held the phone up and studied it as it rang. Hillman glanced at Mr. Houston.

"Don't look at me! Answer the damn thing."

"Hello."

On the other end of the line was Brandon, doing his impersonation of the Dark Knight Batman. Brandon roared, "WHERE IS HE?!"

The collected but confused reverend responded, "Excuse me."

"WHERE IS HE?!"

"Who do you need to speak with, sir?"

"Uh, Dallas."

Reverend Hillman handed Mr. Houston the phone.

"What do you want?"

"The reverend is trying to set you up."

Mr. Houston smashed the phone to the ground, then drew his gun on Reverend Hillman again. "The drop was short. Full of counterfeit bills. Do you care to explain yourself?"

"Earlier today, a homeless guy ran off and attempted to steal one of our packages of money. And a former employee who was randomly in the area returned it. He kissed me on the cheek and ran off. I believe it was Brandon."

Mr. Houston knocked everything off Reverend Hillman's desk in a chaotic rage. "He is done!" Mr. Houston shouted, storming out of the office.

CHAPTER 33

Karla and Steve Bueller, CEO of the "Bueller & Co." CPA accounting firm, finished up an interview.

A disheveled Emily entered the conference room and stared off, disengaged with the world around her.

"Karla, I would like you to meet our rock star, Emily. Thank you, Emily, for joining today," Bueller said.

A distraught Emily nodded her head and manufactured a fractured smile. Her makeup was half done, and the mascara under her eyes appeared to have been running.

"Your dedication to the company is very much appreciated." Bueller turned to Emily. "Karla is our newest hire, and she will be assisting us with the Houston case."

Emily and Karla greeted each other.

"Now, what other discrepancies did we encounter as of lately?" Bueller asked.

"I think we can move forward with the investigation," Karla said. "Mr. Houston's large donations to the church for various unknown charities were used to avoid paying taxes, and there is enough evidence to prove it in court. I dropped off the folder Mr. Houston gave me of the false financial statements Agent Thurman requested this morning. It is now up to the district attorney to press charges."

"That's excellent news," Bueller said as his phone rang. "Excuse me, ladies. My wife's pregnant, and she's due any minute. I must take this." Bueller exited the office.

Emily shielded her face as she attempted to fight back the tears. Karla grabbed a box of Kleenex and moved her chair close to Emily.

"Are you okay? Is there anything I can do for you?"

"No, but thank you. I am sorry that you are meeting me for the first time like this. But my fiancé broke off our engagement days away from our wedding," Emily said as she tried to fight off the tears. "We were supposed to move in together, but he moved all of my things out of his place into a new apartment across town."

"What an asshole?!" Karla said as she placed an arm around Emily. "If I were you, I would find his car, bust out the windows, and slice his tires."

Emily chuckled through the tears. "I'll be fine. What's meant for me will be?" Emily said as a tear rolled down her cheek.

"You should come out with me, tonight."

"I don't know."

"You've been through a lot, and from what I have heard, you have been on this case for weeks. Come out with me. Clear your head. Let's have some fun. We'll do happy hour someplace. I have a housewarming party I was invited to and you could be my plus one."

"That sounds fun, but I don't want to impose."

"You won't. Trust me."

"You know what, why not? Let's do it."

"Yay," Karla said. "This will give us a chance to bond."

Bueller returned. "Sorry about that, ladies," he said. "Let's press forward."

CHAPTER 34

Welcome to Southern Highland located west of Henderson. It is a southern suburb of Las Vegas. Southern Highlands was also where Victor Michaels purchased his home and where the housewarming party commenced. The home was naturally lit and brought out the tone of the home with its modern fixtures.

Shontae was casually dressed, but her outfit was elegant. Her hair and nails were impeccably done. Victor was dressed in a button-down shirt with the sleeves rolled up. Shontae moved around the room efficiently, but she was hurried as she showed a mix of excitement and nervousness before the guests arrived.

Shontae arranged a platter for appetizers on the kitchen island bar. There was cheese, crackers, and fruit assorted to visually please their guests. Victor was busy setting up plates and silverware on the dining table.

"I hope we have enough food for everyone," said Shontae.

Victor walked over and grabbed a can of beer out of the refrigerator. He took a seat at the table, cracked the can open, took a sip, and studied Shontae for a few moments.

"What's your deal?" Shontae asked. "You've been acting weird the last couple of days."

"That is because you have been acting weird the last couple of days."

"Victor, I lost my job. How do you expect me to act?"

"I'm just checking, babe," he said as he walked over and kissed Shontae on the forehead.

"Besides, it's our first time hosting in the new place, and I want everything to be perfect."

The doorbell rang, catching them by surprise. They exchanged a quick, excited glance and kiss. Victor scurried off for the door.

Victor took in a deep breath, reached for the handle, and opened the door to welcome their first guests. It was Karla and Emily.

"Hey, Victor," Karla said as she leaned in for a hug. "This is my new coworker, Emily."

"Nice to meet you," Emily said, as she extended her hand for a greeting.

"Shontae's in the kitchen. Follow me."

"Victor, I love your home. This is a beautiful place," Karla said.

"Thank you," Victor responded as he led the ladies to the living room where Shontae was fluffing the pillows on the couch. "Look who I've found," Victor said to Shontae.

"Karly!" Shontae shouted with pure joy. Excited to see her friend, Shontae ran over to greet Karla with a hug.

"This is Emily. Emily, meet my bestie, Shontae."

"I know you," Shontae said to Emily. "Good to see you again."

Shontae and Emily hugged each other.

"Pleasure seeing you again, Shontae," Emily said as she scanned the room. "Can I borrow your bathroom?"

"Sure. Please make yourself at home," Shontae said. "I'll show you where it's at."

The doorbell rang again.

"And I'll get the door," Victor said.

Shontae and Emily walked off.

Karla walked to the kitchen, where she found an open bottle of wine sitting on the table. She grabbed a glass and poured herself some. Karla got excited as she gazed out one of the kitchen windows and saw Justice's car had just pulled up.

CHAPTER 35

Brandon and I scooped out of the place from a parking space on the other side of the street a few feet away from Victor's home. Justice had pulled up on the curb. He exited his car and headed toward the front door. Justice's left hand seemed to be wrapped extensively in a brace.

"There is Justice. Let's go in," Brandon suggested.

Brandon tried to open the door, but I locked it.

"Let me out."

"Not yet," I said as I scrolled through my phone and found the contact number to the payday loan center I was at a few days ago where I had met a woman named Monica.

"Hello, Payday Loans," the receptionist said. "How may I help you today?"

"Hello, may I speak to Monica."

"This is she. Who do I have the pleasure of speaking with?"

"My name is Terrence. I walked into your store a couple of days ago. Not sure if you remember me?"

"Terrence?" Monica questioned. "Were you the guy with a 99 credit score?"

"Sure. Yeah. So, I was wondering if you could meet me someplace?"

"Meet you someplace? Like on a date?"

"Kinda, sorta. Not really. It's at Victor's new home."

"Victor's new home?"

"Haven't you heard? He bought a new home, and he's throwing a housewarming party. Weren't you invited?"

"I was not."

"Well, consider this an invite, darling. I'll forward you the location. I have a plan, and I'll explain it to you once you get here." A shit-eating grin splashed across my face as I ended the call.

CHAPTER 36

Victor peeked through the peephole to see an anxious Justice pacing back and forth as he waited outside the door.

Victor opened the door. "What's up, my man? Glad you could make it," Victor said and he extended his hand.

Justice extended his good hand as he tried to conceal his heavily bandaged one.

"You good, homey? What happened to your hand?"

"I'm fine."

"Cool. Come in. My brother and his girl arrived just before you. They should be in the living room. Follow me," Victor said as he guided Justice through the beautiful modern home.

They made their way into the living room to see Darius and Denice in the middle of a weird rock, paper, scissor war.

"Darius and Denice, this is Justice."

Darius turned around. Justice's eyes widened as he quickly remembered Darius from the Taste of Rainbow club and it stunned the both of them. The doorbell rang.

"I'll be right back," said Victor. Victor sped off.

Darius furrowed a brow as he extended his hand to Justice. Darius asked, "Have we crossed paths before?"

"Weren't you at Taste—"

"Yes! I remember you," Darius said cutting Justice off from completing his statement. "Good to see you again." He continued as he leaned close. "Keep that between us."

"I thought I heard your voice," Karla said as she entered the living room. She walked up and attempted to kiss the standoffish Justice. "What's with you?"

"We need to talk," Justice said sternly.

CHAPTER 37

A half-hour later, Brandon knocked on the door as I stood several feet away, obscuring Victor's view of me.

The door opened.

"What's up, man?" Brandon said as he awkwardly hugged Victor.

"Long time," Victor said.

"I know."

"Karla and the girls are in the kitchen.

"Wait, Karla's here?" Brandon said as he scurried off into the house before a proper invitation into it.

Victor waited at the door for a few seconds as he watched me strut forward with my arm around Monica. Victor's jaw dropped as he tried to avoid eye contact with Monica.

"Wait," Monica said. "You got something on your lips."

Monica planted a fat, long, wet petty kiss on my lips. Oh, my, and yes there was a little bit of tongue action involved. Monica walked through the entrance. Victor stared me down as I followed up behind.

Monica entered the kitchen with the ladies. "Hey, everyone."

Shontae was the first one to greet Monica. "Hi, I'm Shontae. Victor's girlfriend."

"Victor's girlfriend," she said as she scanned Shontae up and down. "Interesting." Monica kept her cool.

Emily waved from a distance as she sat alone in her thoughts.

"Everyone, take a seat at the table. The food is almost done. I'll gather everyone else," Shontae said as she scurried out of the room.

~

Justice and Karla were in a heated conversation in one of Victor's guest rooms.

"He promised me this beautiful life," Karla said. "But he took advantage of me. And ironically now, I started dating his stepson. And that is another story for another day."

"Why didn't you tell me?"

"Because it's complicated and it was none of your business."

"Well, it became my business when he broke my hand and put a gun to my head."

Shontae stuck her head in the room. "There you are."

There was an awkward pause between Justice and Shontae. This was the first time they had seen each other since the firing.

"Justice," Shontae said, acknowledging his presence.

"Shontae! Hey, it's been a minute, huh?"

"By a minute do you mean a couple of days ago?" Shontae said with a fake smile.

"Close enough," Justice said.

"Girl, the food is ready," Shontae said as she rolled her eyes at Justice and walked off.

"I keep forgetting Shontae and Victor are a thing."

"Can we talk about all of this a little later?"

Justice nodded and they followed behind Shontae.

∼

In the living room, the stare-down between Victor and me continued.

"It's pitiful how bad you really try to be in my shoes," said Victor.

"From the way things appear, you're in my shoes. You got my ol' lady, and you got the promotion I turned down. Congrats on coming in second again."

Shontae and Karla entered the living room, and Shontae froze once she saw me.

"The food is ready."

Victor grabbed Shontae's butt and shamelessly placed his arm around her to taunt me.

Shontae pushed his arm off her. "Do not ever do that again!" Shontae said sternly.

"That's what you get, fool," I said with a chuckle.

"You're both acting like pathetic little boys."

"That's not on me," I said in defense. "Victor can't handle our past."

Shontae shot me a glare of disgust, before she stormed off to the kitchen. Victor and I followed up right behind.

CHAPTER 38

Everyone made their way to the dinner table and found a seat next to their significant other.

Ben, an ex-coworker, popped up out of nowhere, and bear-hugged me. "Terrence! Hey man, how have you been?"

"Good," I said.

"You silly fuck. You're the only person in history to quit a job before getting a promotion."

"Yeah, I've heard."

"You gotta meet my fiancé," Ben said. "Babe, get over here. I want you to meet someone."

Cynthia walked over to me and reintroduced herself as if we had never met a couple of nights before at the casino suite. Through the awkward greeting, we managed to not make it weird. I scanned the table, and I noticed someone staring at the side of my face. "Denice? Hey," I said. "Hey, Brandon. Check out who's here."

Brandon got on a knee next to Karla and appeared to be professing his love. He lifted his head and noticed Denice waving at him. He stood and made eye contact with me. "Oh, shit! Denice from the strip—"

"Yes! The Strip," Denice said, interrupting Brandon. "We met on the Strip, remember?" She nodded to encourage Brandon on the deflection.

"Oh, yes. We met on the Strip. Right. Yes, the Strip," Brandon said, not blowing Denice's cover.

I shrugged. Brandon and I were the only ones that knew Denice was a stripper.

Ben was in a severe state of cogitation. "Now that I'm thinking about it, Denice, I think I've seen you on that part of the Strip before."

Apparently, Ben had seen Denice at the same strip club. All the anxiety-ridden Denice could do was generate a fake smile as she nodded her head.

Also sitting at the table was Emily, who was seated next to the lady in the red dress, whose name, I think, was Karla.

Interesting, I thought.

Justice entered the room and froze once he noticed Emily seated at the table. By now it was too late. Emily got up from the table and charged right at him.

"I can't believe I loved you, Justice. Couldn't you tell me face-to-face? Seriously? Facebook messenger? You couldn't have sent a text or, better yet, break our engagement off in person?"

"Can we talk about this someplace else?"

"Why? So, you can make amends over Snapchat?"

Karla stood from the table and made her way to Justice. "You guys know each other?"

"Oh my God!" Emily said as she was inches away from breaking into tears. "I'm guessing you were the reason he called off our engagement."

"Wait! What are you talking about?"

"This was the guy who broke my heart."

Karla was at a loss for words. Her body language told Emily everything she needed to know about Justice and Karla's entanglement. All of a sudden, Emily smacked Justice in the face. She grabbed her things from the table and stormed out of the house.

The whole room grew quiet as Karla and Justice took their seats at the table and everyone settled in their places. Plates were passed around as we all got ready to feast on the dinner. Suddenly, the doorbell rang again.

"Are we expecting more people?" Shontae asked Victor.

Victor shrugged.

"It's probably Dallas," said Denice.

Justice choked on his drink.

"You know Dallas, too?" Brandon said with concern.

"Well, yeah. He's my father."

Brandon became jittery as Justice attempted to hide his nervousness. The doorbell rang again and again and again.

"I'll get it," Denice said as she stood from the table and exited the room.

Brandon began to stuff his face with food. "Terrence, we might have to leave."

"Why?" My phone vibrated. I dug my phone out of my pocket and received a text in all caps from Justice that read, *WE HAVE TO LEAVE.*

Moments later, Denice returned to the room with none other than Becca, the big girl from the molly-infused threesome.

We all caught the tail-end of their conversation. "And daddy was being an asshole to me," Becca complained.

"Language please," a frustrated Denice said as they approached the dinner table. "Hey, everyone, this is my baby sister, Becca," said Denice, introducing us.

Brandon choked on his food. "Wait...Dallas is your father, too?"

"Yeah. Why do you care, Ass Face?"

"Ass Face?" Brandon questioned. He leaned over and whispered to Justice, "I didn't stick my face in that, did I?"

"You sure did, Ass Face," Becca said as she overheard Brandon's question.

"Watch your mouth, Rebecca," Denice said sternly.

I took a sip of my drink.

"I can say whatever I want to," said Becca. "I'm almost eighteen years old."

I gagged on my drink.

CHAPTER 39

Some time passed as everyone got comfortable at the table. Private conversations were going on around Justice, Brandon, Victor, and me. I am not sure what was going on in Brandon's or Justice's heads. I know what is going through Victor's head because I currently lived in it. He had not taken his scowl off me since I had entered his home. Now was the time to *Set It Off* like Queen Latifah. I leaned toward Brandon and mumbled, "I saw this on TV once." I picked up my fork and tapped my wine glass until the conversations around the table stopped. This was also a cue for Monica to speak.

"Shontae, is it?" Monica asked. "How long have you and Victor been dating?"

"A little under a year," Shontae said.

Victor interrupted. "Before there are any more disruptions," he started as he grabbed Shontae's hand and stood to his feet. "Words can't explain the way I feel about you. I knew you were my forever a few years ago when we were friends. You've been with me through thick and thin, and I hope our bond is stronger than anything that tries to destroy it," he said, directing his energy at me. "I love you," Victor said as he made eye contact with Shontae Hillman. He dropped to one knee, pulled out a small box, and opened it to reveal a big diamond ring. "Will you marry me?"

Shontae paused a second. "Yes!"

Everyone except for Monica and me erupted in a volcanic outburst of excitement and cheer as the newly engaged couple kissed each other.

Brandon waited for everyone to calm down from the emotional high of the proposal. He got to his feet. "There's something I want to say." He took the floor.

This fool upstaged me, delaying all the plans I had. I was hoping Brandon would not do what I thought he was about to do.

"When a boy turns into a man, they should already know what they want and when they want it." Brandon approached Karla. He pulled out a box and dropped down to a knee. "Karla, will you—"

I rushed over, put Brandon in a headlock, and dragged him into another room.

"Ouch! Let me go," Brandon said as he struggled to get loose from my hold.

"Monica, can I see you in the other room as well?" I said as I dragged Brandon out of the dining room.

Monica followed behind us.

"What's your deal?" Brandon asked.

"What's my deal? Fool, you made an audible. How are you gonna upstage me like that? You knew what the damn plan was. We went over it in the car."

"I'm sorry. I got caught up in the moment. I just wanted to get mine out of the way," Brandon said.

"Bro, I can't let you do that."

"Why? What has love ever done to you? You love hater."

"I am not a love hater. It has nothing to do with love. I just think you're four words away from making an ass out of yourself. Trust me on this."

"Really? Why should I? What happened?"

"I can't say it. I'm already violating the Guy Code tonight. I can't do it twice in one day."

"Tell me," Brandon pleaded. "What is going on?"

"I don't wanna feel like a bitch."

"You're being a bitch by not telling me. Either say what it is, or I'm gonna go propose to my girl."

"Brandon, she's not for you."

"How do you know?" Brandon said as he waited for me to answer.

I remained silent.

Brandon sighed and started to walk back into the dining area.

"Okay. Fine, fool! Truth or dare."

"Truth or dare?"

"Yeah."

"Okay, dare."

"You were supposed to take the truth route," I said and thought on it a moment. "Okay. I dare you not to tell Justice I told you he's been sleeping with Karla."

Brandon thought on it a second and stormed off. I turned my attention to Monica.

"Why are you tiptoeing? Go for the throat."

"I can't do it," Monica said.

"But we had a deal," I said. "You were supposed to help me get my girl back, and I pay you to get back at a guy who has been playing you."

"I know, but it doesn't feel right."

"Politicians get paid to lie. I'm paying you to tell the truth."

There was an uproar in the kitchen.

We rushed back to the kitchen. Brandon was in the middle of confronting Justice.

"It doesn't matter who told me. I'm just glad that Terrence is a real friend."

"Wow, thanks, Brandon."

Brandon crept closer to Justice.

"I didn't know you two were involved."

WHAM! Brandon caught Justice off guard with a blow to the cheek. The impact knocked Justice to the ground.

The force from the punch shocked even Brandon, and he rushed out of the house expecting Justice to recover and retaliate. Justice stood and stormed off after Brandon.

Monica re-entered the quiet kitchen. "Shontae, me and your new fiancé have been sleeping with each other for the last six months. And I'm pregnant with his child."

I smacked the table with excitement. "Checkmate, bitch," I shouted as I downed my drink and headed for the exit.

"Terrence, wait," Shontae said.

Was this the moment? I thought as Shontae approached me. It was almost as if she was moving toward me in slow motion. It felt like it was one of the many dream sequences I had envisioned of her running into my arms. I could not believe I was about to win back over my Shontae's heart.

"Did you bring her to my house?"

"I thought you needed to know who you were really dealing with."

"Are you a child?"

"Wait, you're mad at me? I'm the wrong person—"

SMACK! Shontae slapped my face. "Stay the fuck out of my life." Shontae ran to the back. Victor chased after her. *With the victory, there was also defeat,* I thought as I walked out of the house.

Darius stared out of the window by the kitchen sink.

"These guys are silly," Darius said.

Denice approached the window and watched as Justice chased Brandon around a car as the fight continued outside. "Who knew there would be so much drama tonight?"

"I'm glad we're honest with each other, babe," Darius said as he kissed Denice on the forehead. Denice produced a fake smile.

Meanwhile, everybody was outside of the house at this point. Justice chased Brandon around a car until, eventually, Justice outsmarted Brandon and got a chance to get his hands on him. I spectated for a few moments as Justice slammed Brandon to the ground. The two continued to wrestle until I decided to break it up.

Suddenly, *SMACK!* I caught a wild punch to the face. "Ah, hell no." I took off my belt and swung wildly, hitting any and everything that was in sight. "Brandon, get your ass in the car!"

"You ain't the boss of me," Brandon said.

I swung the belt at Brandon, and he dodged, finally heading in the direction of my vehicle as I chased after him.

Moments later, *CRUNCH!* Emily had jumped on the hood of Justice's Corvette and smashed his windshield with a big ass brick. "Thanks for the advice, Karla," Emily said. She proceeded to slice Justice's tires. "I'll see you in child support court," she said after she sliced the last tire and walked off into the desert night.

CHAPTER 40

The car ride was somber as Brandon and I rode alone into the night. We both sat in our thoughts, reflecting on the series of events that transpired at the dinner party we had crashed earlier that evening. There was not much to say because we made complete asses out of ourselves in front of the women we loved. Sometimes, men think like boys and make immature decisions.

The empty fuel light appeared on the dashboard of my car. I pulled the car over into the nearest gas station and parked by a gas pump. I shut off the engine and sat in my thoughts a little longer.

"I thought exposing Victor would help me win Shontae back," I said out loud to myself. "But it backfired. Now I'm all sentimotional like a Drake song."

"I've done a lot of things that I'm so ashamed of, but this takes the cake."

"You shouldn't be ashamed of yourself, that's your parents' job," I said as I glanced to the backseat where we had all our money. "We just need to get the money first. Once we have that, then get the woman."

"Amen to that," Brandon said. He sighed as he stared out of the window into the starlit night sky. "I'm always getting caught up with women that don't want me like I want them. Did you know my first girlfriend left me for a guy in a college dress?"

"A guy in a college dress?" I said as my face contorted. I turned and stared at Brandon. "Did you mean a gynecologist, fool?"

"Oh! That is how you say it?"

"See, Brandon! That is probably why she left you. You're third-world ignorant."

"Just continue to kick me in the balls while I'm already down, Terrence."

"My bad, fam! Hurt people, hurt people sometimes," I said with a sigh. "Let's get this cash to my mom and get the hell out of town before something else crazy happens."

"Don't put that energy out into the universe," he said as he looked to the sky and pleaded. "He didn't mean it."

I stared at Brandon with confusion for a few seconds. "I'll never forget the first time we met, but I'll keep trying to forget."

"You did it again, bro."

"My bad," I said as I stepped out of the car and walked into the store.

∼

Seconds passed as Brandon sat in the car. Suddenly, someone entered from the back of the vehicle, struck Brandon in the head with the butt of a pistol, and placed the gun to Brandon's temple. It was Mr. Houston. "Move over and drive," he said.

Brandon moved over to the driver's seat, put the seat belt on, cranked the engine, and drove off.

Minutes passed as Brandon drove as Mr. Houston's hostage.

"Where are we going?"

Mr. Houston struck Brandon in the head again.

"Shut your mouth before I fuck it," Mr. Houston said.

"I can't believe you kiss my mother with lips that utter words like that."

"I can't believe I've kissed your mother with all the dicks she's sucked."

Brandon thought about it for a second. "You got me there."

Mr. Houston struck Brandon in the head again. "Shut up! You've fucked me over for the last time, and now you'll die for it."

Brandon peeped at the rear-view mirror and noticed Mr. Houston was not wearing a seat belt. Suddenly, Brandon smashed the car brakes.

POP! The gun fired off a round.

Mr. Houston flew forward into the dashboard. Brandon hopped out of the vehicle and dashed off, leaving the car in the middle of the street.

POP. POP. POP. POP. POP. POP. POP. CLICK. CLICK. Mr. Houston emptied the clip. He looked to the back seat and noticed a duffel bag.

Brandon was in a full panicky sprint as he hauled ass through an empty park.

∼

Meanwhile, I was at the gas station wondering where the hell Brandon went with my damn car. Nonetheless I realized, *Brandon got me for the loot.*

I dug in my pocket to call the cops, but Brandon was calling simultaneously.

"Yo," a winded Brandon said.

"What are you doing, fool?"

"Running!"

"Running!? Why are you running? Where the hell is my car?"

Brandon stopped running. "Fuck."

"What the fuck does 'fuck' mean? The money was in the car, Brandon. Where the fuck is the car?"

"OH NO! OKAY! Give me a minute to figure it out," Brandon said as he started to jog back toward the area of the car.

"My car has an anti-theft tracking device on. I'll just go report it as stolen."

"No. They'll find the money and the fake bills. Meet me at my mom's bar. It's right up the street."

~

Brandon hung up the phone and returned to the car's last location. He paused mid step as he stared at the empty stretch of asphalt. Brandon swallowed hard as he tried to catch his breath. He patted his pockets in search of Terrence's car keys. He felt nothing and shouted, "Fuck!"

Brandon scanned the surrounding area and found nothing. His heartbeat quickened as the sickening realization dawned on him. Terrence's car was missing, as was all of the money he had worked so hard to obtain.

CHAPTER 41

I had been pacing back and forth at the damn club for almost an hour, wondering how the hell this fool lost my car. A big, burly wicked-looking security guard with an intimidating demeanor approached me and asked, "You all right, mate?"

"I'm good. Just waiting on someone."

"OK. Please don't block the entrance," the security guard said.

My phone rang. I screened the call, then answered, "Hey, Mom."

"Terrence, two big guys are banging on the door. What do I do?" she said, panicky with a whisper.

"Don't answer it! Go hide."

"Oh my God! What's happening, Terrence?"

"Make sure you don't answer any unknown numbers or answer the door. I'll take care of it."

Brandon finally arrived as he walked through the entrance.

"It's about damn time," I said. "We need to get out of here."

"Have you seen Jessie?" Brandon asked.

"No, did you get the car back?"

"I'll have to get you another one."

"What about the money?"

"It's gone. Dallas Houston took it."

My heart sank. How would I be able to help my parents out of their jam now that the money was gone?

Brandon dug into his pocket, pulled out his phone, and screened the call. "It's him," Brandon said as he answered the call. "Where is the car, Dallas?"

"Thanks for holding on to my money," Mr. Houston said. "Now, I'm gonna go fuck your mother like you tried to fuck me." The call ended.

"We have to go," Brandon said.

"How," I said. "We have no means of transportation." I shook my head. "Just go do whatever. I'll walk home."

As I walked out of the bar and into the night, I had one thought in my head. We were so close but now so far. How would I be able to help my family out of this jam?

CHAPTER 42

In the modest but stylish apartment's living room, the ceiling fan twirled in the dim sun setting through the blinds. The energy in the room was anything but calm. Karla was in a loose sweater with leggings and was curled up on the couch. She stared blankly at her phone.

Her father, Roger Hernandez, paced back and forth as his face weathered with concern. The weight of reality had sunk in as Roger stopped pacing and sat on the armrest of the couch. "You know egomaniac guys like that don't like to be crossed," he said as he broke the silence.

"I didn't think he would go this far, Papi," Karla said her voice soft as she rubbed her temples. "I didn't cross him. I wasn't myself with him. He was trying to control and manipulate my life. And now he's threatening to take away everything. My apartment, the car… even your house."

"Men like that use money as a weapon. He's used to getting everything he wants and when he doesn't get it, he tries to make whoever's life miserable."

Karla shook her head as her eyes welled up. "I thought I was in control. I met a guy I liked, but he's involved with another woman I just found out I work with. I just can't get it together, Papi," Karla said as tears started to spill over. "Where do I go from here?"

Roger's posture straightened up as his face hardened up with quiet resolve. "I've lived a lot of life, Karla. We will figure this out. I have had my fair share of dealing with bullies. He is a coward that is not invincible. I will not let anything happen to you," Roger said.

"But what if he comes after you? I could not live with myself," she said.

"Whatever happens, we'll face it together. I'll sell the damn house, if need be," Roger said. "We'll find a way. We always have, and always will."

"I'm sorry it's come to this. I know you loved your house and I don't want you to lose it," said Karla. "You've worked so hard your whole life and I—"

"Don't apologize," Roger said. "I'll be fine. You did the right thing, baby girl. I am proud of you."

"Thanks, Papi. I don't deserve you," Karla said as she wiped her eyes.

"Maybe not, but I'll always be here for you," Roger said with a smile.

The two of them embraced.

There was a knock at the door. A concerned Roger stood to his feet. Karla rushed to the door and took a quick glimpse through the peephole.

"It's OK," she said.

"I need to use the shower," Roger said and walked to the back of the apartment.

Karla opened the door, and it was a dejected yet humbled Justice with his head hung low.

"My apologies for tonight," Justice said. "I didn't know you and Emily worked together."

"At this point, does it matter?"

"I guess not."

They each waited for the other to speak.

"I know, at first, we started out by hooking up. But my feelings for you have grown," Justice said. "The reason tonight happened was because of my genuine feelings for you."

"Don't you think you could've communicated that a little better than you did? Emily didn't deserve that."

"It was a very immature action. She deserved better communication from me."

"What if you and I had become something? How would I know you wouldn't treat me like you did Emily?"

"I wasn't in love with her," Justice said. "But Karla, I'm in love with"

A toilet flushed in the background, interrupting Justice's sentence. Roger shouted, "Baby, where are the towels?"

Before Karla could explain, Justice ran off like a kid who took his basketball home after a loss.

"Justice! Wait!" Karla said.

CHAPTER 43

I entered the apartment and noticed Justice on the couch nursing his bruised left black eye he had received from the fight with Brandon.

A few moments later, Brandon entered.

Justice stood and the two of them squared off as if they were about to fight again. I stood back and out of the way. If they were about to get into it again, I was just going to stand back and watch the fireworks.

"Why are you at my place?"

Brandon turned to me and said, "I'm not talking to Justice. Can you tell him to go fuck himself and stay the hell away from my sister?"

"I'm pretty sure he heard you," I responded.

"I called it off, Brandon. Emily deserves better."

"Can you tell that asshole 'Thank you'?"

"Leave me alone," I said to them both. "It's both of y'alls fault all of this shit happened to me."

Brandon received a FaceTime video call. It was an emotional Jessica with two black eyes. "Jessie! What happened? Where are you?"

"The police station," Jessica said. "Dallas has gone mad. He's going to kill you if he sees you again."

"Are you okay?"

"Don't worry about me. I have to go now," Jessica said and hung up.

Brandon headed for the door. "I have to talk with Dallas."

"What's to talk about? Your mother just said he's going to kill you."

"I have to get that car back," Brandon said.

"Fuck that car. That Dallas dude seems crazy."

"Yeah, he is," Justice said as he lifted his arm. "He broke my hand."

"Maybe you deserved it," Brandon said with a little snark.

"That's fair," Justice said in response.

Brandon dug in his pocket, pulled out an envelope, and handed it to me. "I need you to hold on to this. When the time comes, I will let you know when to open it," Brandon said, exiting the apartment.

I sat in my thoughts for a few moments.

"You okay?" Justice asked.

"It was right there, Justice. I had the money to help my mother."

Justice received a phone call. "Hold that thought," Justice said. "What do you want, Karla? Oh… I'm sorry, I didn't know that was your father." Justice walked out of the condo.

I kicked off my shoes and fell asleep on the couch.

CHAPTER 44

Special Agent Leslie Thurman sat at her desk in the FBI's Las Vegas field office, her eyes immersed in the complicated web pinned to the corkboard of the crime tree in front of her. Photos, papers, and red ribbons led a complicated road to the last man standing where the counterfeiting bills were coming from: Lorenzo Carlucci. Lorenzo was the underworld's puppet master, controlling an empire of immorality and evil.

Leslie had spent months building a case against Lorenzo, pulling together evidence from several investigations. She had examined bank documents, reviewed surveillance footage, and questioned informants in hopes of destroying Lorenzo's illegal network. She was the point guard leading her team in taking him down.

The key had been tracking the money. Hundreds of thousands of counterfeit dollars had flooded Las Vegas, each one a possible clue that led back to Lorenzo. Leslie's breakthrough came when she linked a lump sum of counterfeit bills to Lorenzo's loan sharking operations and, just recently, a strip club called The Velvet Room. The club was known as a hotbed for illegal activity.

As she paced the floor, Leslie's phone rang, jolting her out of her thoughts. It was her partner, Special Agent Mike Lawson.

"Hey, Les, you ready for tonight?" Mike asked, his voice bursting with enthusiasm.

"As ready as I'll ever be," Leslie responded, as she stared at the clock. It was almost time to relocate.

Tonight was the night they would take down Lorenzo. The operation, a well-planned trap intended to capture Lorenzo in the act, had been months in the works. Leslie had her squad in place, with each spy briefed and ready to do risky cop work.

Leslie and Mike prepared to leave as the sun began to drop above the city, creating sweeping shadows across the desert terrain. They drove quietly, the anxiety hanging heavy in the air. Leslie's mind raced, going over every detail to ensure nothing had been forgotten.

They arrived at The Velvet Room, blending in with the crowds of customers lined up outside. Neon lights swirled overhead, illuminating the club's flashy facade. Inside, the air was dense with smoke and the throbbing sounds of electronic music. Leslie and Mike proceeded through the packed room, watching for any signs of danger.

Lorenzo and his lieutenants sat in a secret room in the back of the club, counting stacks of money. He was unaware of the trap about to ensnare him as he was confident in his untouchable status. Leslie watched from a secret vantage point, her heart racing as the moment neared.

Leslie gave Mike a nod and indicated to the crew. Agents acted quickly, securing exits and establishing their positions. Leslie took a deep breath, bracing herself for the encounter ahead. She pushed through the door, holding her badge high and her pistol pointed at Carlucci.

"FBI! Everyone, freeze where you are!" Leslie yelled, her voice breaking over the music and chatter.

Lorenzo's men hurried to react, causing chaos to break out. Lorenzo froze, his eyes fixed on Leslie with a mix of disbelief and wrath.

"You've got to be kidding me," Lorenzo mumbled, automatically grabbing for the mounds of cash on the table.

"Lorenzo Carlucci, you're under arrest for counterfeiting, loan sharking, and solicitation of prostitution," Leslie declared as she stepped forward. "It is over, Lorenzo. We got you."

Lorenzo's expression curled in defiance. "These charges are bogus. I'll be out before the night is over," he said with a chuckle as he stared down Leslie. "I'm not sure you know who you're dealing with, sweetheart."

Leslie remained firm. "I know exactly who I'm dealing with. And I have all of the proof I need to lock you up."

Leslie felt a sense of accomplishment when agents handcuffed Lorenzo and his men. Months of hard labor had finally paid off. She had tracked the money and discovered the truth; now, justice would be served.

Leslie returned to the office, where she began writing her last report. The weight of the night's events began to sink in, as did a sense of accomplishment. She had demolished Lorenzo's enterprise piece by piece and removed a dangerous criminal from the streets.

Leslie took one last glance at the corkboard, her network of links complete. She had made a difference in the fight against crime.

CHAPTER 45

I did not sleep a wink. I hate this expensive fucking couch. When I get my spot, I will get a sofa that loves me more than my mother. Why was the damn TV on? I guess I had forgotten to turn it off before I went to sleep. I do not remember leaving the TV on, though. I rolled over and noticed a pale-faced, teary-eyed Justice being comforted by Karla on the other end of the couch. They both stared at the TV.

"Fuck Terrence's sleeping ass, huh!" I said with angered sarcasm. "You guys couldn't find a better place to be sentimotional at?"

"You have to see this," Justice said as he rewound the television.

A news anchor from the KTNV Las Vegas local news said, "Last night, a body was found in the trunk of a torched Lincoln limousine registered to Dallas Houston. Dental records identified the body to be the remains of Brandon Perez. Houston was detained moments later after fleeing the scene of a stolen vehicle."

"Are you serious?" I said, staring at the screen in disbelief.

We sat for several moments in disbelief. Moments later, I noticed Justice and Karla making kissy faces as if the news of Brandon happened months ago.

"We're heading out of town for a little bit," Justice said as he stood to his feet. He turned to Karla. "Can you give us a minute? I'll meet you in the car." Justice dug in his pocket and handed her his car keys.

"All of this is kinda hard to swallow. I can't believe Brandon's dead."

"People come and go in your life for a reason," Justice said.

"Yeah, I guess."

"If I sold my rental houses and the condo, that would put me a little over one point one million on paper. So technically speaking, I have already won," Justice said. "You don't have to bow or send me any money for the bet. Just wanted to give you a heads up."

"Are you a fucking sociopath? Even through death, you are keeping a scoreboard. Our childhood friend died, and you're coming to me about a stupid bet?"

"You're right. My timing was off."

I stared Justice down for a few moments. "I think it's time for me to move out, bro. We've been roommates since we were teenagers. We're not boys anymore. We're men now. It's time we stand on our own."

"Karla and I are heading to Cabo," Justice said. "Wanna come?"

I shook my head. "With what money," I said. "You two have fun."

We hugged and went our separate ways. Moments later, I received a phone call from Nicole but I ignored it. I noticed I had several missed calls from my mother, Shontae, and Nicole, and a few missed messages from Brandon. On the television, Reverend Hillman sermonized.

Brandon's last statement read; *I hope this makes up for me getting your car stolen.* Attached to the message were multiple photos of Reverend Hillman in compromising positions.

CHAPTER 46

I walked up the cobblestone driveway in an affluent neighborhood in Centennial Hills of North Las Vegas. I approached the front door and knocked. A few moments later, Reverand Hillman opened the door. He was not dressed to impress in his usual expensive suits, but he was still fresh. Reverand Hillman's more casual attire was more superior to any average Joe.

"Terrence," Reverend Hillman said as he nervously scanned the neighborhood. "To what pleasure do I owe your visit?"

"You mind if we speak in private?" I asked.

Reverend Hillman was hesitant, at first, as he stared down at me. "Sure," Reverend Hillman said, guiding me through his home. We walked past a stacked stone fireplace in the living room. I always remembered how this place was magnificently constructed. We entered his office, and I sat right across from him. He took a seat at his desk.

"So, how can I help you?"

"I'm starting a GoFundMe for a new TV show I wanted to produce here in town. I could use your support."

The reverend took a moment to respond. "What's the show about?"

"I'm glad you asked. It's about shady preachers and the people they've manipulated."

Reverend Hillman studied me for a few more seconds. "For what aspect of this project is my support warranted?"

I took a pen and a piece of paper from his desk and wrote $250,000 on it. I slid it across the desk to Reverend Hillman.

"What's this?" Reverend Hillman asked, studying the paper.

"It's my pitch. You once said an ambitious man should always have a pitch. So, there it is."

"So, two-hundred fifty grand is your pitch?"

"Yes. On my way to your house, I stopped by Walgreens and printed out a few images I thought would solidify my pitch," I tossed a large envelope on Reverend Hillman's desk.

The preacher hesitated a moment. He reached for the envelope and opened the folder. Inside the envelope were some random photos of him with the fake prostitutes we hung out with a few nights ago on the Strip.

"Let us pray," I said as I bowed my head. "Lord, I've sinned in the City of Sin. I plan to use these pictures as blackmail to throw Reverend Hillman under the spiritual bus. I know about his operation of laundering money through the church while also misleading people in your name. I plan to become economically stable and maybe one day, if she's open to it, marry Reverend Hillman's daughter, Shontae. And if he has any clue what I'm going to do with these photos if he ever tries to stop me, I ask that you bless him with the awareness and discernment to cough up the cash. Amen." I opened my eyes to see a puzzled Reverend Hillman. I rose up from the desk and it was my turn to stare down on the fake-ass reverend.

"What is the routing and checking account number to your bank?" Reverend Hillman said.

Check and Mate! I thought as a smug smile grew across my face.

CHAPTER 47

I arrived back at the condo and took a seat on the couch. I pulled out my phone and checked my dating apps. I had received a few more matches and messages, including from LesFit. *Let's meet for coffee.*

I typed back, *I have some free time now. Where can I meet you?*

She texted back, *Let's meet at The Writer's Block.*

I replied, *Great. I'm a few blocks away. See you in a few.*

The three dots flashed across the screen, and she responded, *OK, great!*

Suddenly, BOOM! BOOM! BOOM! There was a hard knock at the door, which startled me. I eased up to the door and looked through the peephole. I saw a random police officer staring through the peephole from the other side.

I calmed myself down, then proceeded to open the door a crack. "How can I help you?" The officer held the black duffel bag that had been in my car.

"Are you Terrence Ware?"

"Depends on whose asking. What happened?"

The officer rolled over the bag and suddenly reached for something inside his coat.

I threw my hands up.

The officer grabbed his gun and drew down on me. "What are you doing?" the officer asked.

"I'm putting my damn hands up. Isn't that how this shit goes?"

The officer lowered his gun and placed it back in the holster. He whipped out a badge and flashed it to me. "I'm Detective Saeed Haddad of the Las Vegas Police Department. Your car was found at a crime scene last night and I found a bag in the backseat with about two hundred fifty thousand dollars cash in it. I kept fifty thousand dollars of it. Here's the contact info to pick up your car." The officer handed over a business card. "Pleasure doing business with you, sir."

Confused at what had just happened, I quietly shut the door. I opened the bag and discovered the cash from the church scheme. I grabbed the card the officer handed me and dialed the number on it.

"Vegas Towing Company, how can I help you?"

"Yes, you guys have my vehicle in your possession, and I'd like to have it delivered someplace."

"What's the make and model of the vehicle?"

"It's a 540i BMW."

The receptionist took a moment to search for the information on the car. "Thank you for that information. Where would you like it delivered to?"

"The BMW dealership in Las Vegas."

"Thank you very much."

The phone call ended, and I dialed the dealership.

"Thank you for calling BMW of Las Vegas. Your call is very important to us. If you know your party's extension—"

I pressed zero to get to the operator and waited a few more seconds for the operator to answer.

"BMW Las Vegas, how can I direct your call?"

"I'm returning my vehicle. Who can I speak with?"

"I'll transfer you to the sales department. Please hold the line."

"Thank you."

The first move I needed to make after getting the dough was to get rid of that car that was the biggest liability in my life. I had other plans for the money.

CHAPTER 48

I stepped out of the hot Vegas sun and into the cool inviting atmosphere of The Writer's Block coffee shop. The transition from the hectic downtown streets to the book-lined interior was instantly soothing. I got here before my date to give me time to settle in and scan the place. I chose a table by a window. I glanced at the door, expecting to see her walk in at any moment. There was a light hum of random conversations and the smell of freshly brewed coffee filled the air.

As I settled inside the coffee shop, I received a call from my mother. "Hey, Mom."

"What did you do?" she asked.

"Nothing, why?"

"Two-hundred and fifty thousand dollars mysteriously went into my bank account. Did you rob a bank or something?"

"I didn't rob a bank, Mom. It's all legal, and it's yours," I said as I scanned the room.

"Oh my God. Okay, I have to tithe. I have to give ten percent back to the church."

"Mom, don't worry. I took care of the church. Just enjoy the money."

"Thank you, Jesus. Okay, let me call you back. Love ya."

"Love you, Mom."

The call ended. I got a little caught up in my feelings. Who said money doesn't buy happiness? The excitement in her voice made me happy. I could honestly say that I was at peace for the first time in a while.

Soft music played in the background as I received another incoming phone call. This time the call was a restricted number. I hesitated to answer it, but I figured why not. "Who the hell is this?"

"It's me," the caller said.

"Who the hell is, 'Me?'" I asked.

"What other me would say, 'it's me' without saying who me, is?" the caller said.

I ended the call. I did not have time for dumbass games. But what other dumbass would play these kind of dumbass games? It couldn't be that dumbass though, I thought. It sure sounded like… But could it be? I thought about it for a moment. The unknown caller called back. "Why are you playing on my phone?"

"No joke. It's me."

"Why the hell are you not dead, Brandon?"

"Don't say that name on unsecured lines. It's a long story, but to put it simply, a dead man doesn't pay taxes and life insurance is one of the best investments for someone thought to be deceased."

"So, now you've committed insurance fraud?"

"Don't broadcast it to the whole world, Terrence!"

"My bad, bro! You were on the news. I thought you were dead."

"I can't go into detail at the moment, but, by any chance, do you have that envelope I handed you?"

"I do actually."

"Sweet! OK. Open it."

I dug into my pocket and opened the envelope. It was three tickets from three different sportsbooks. Two were straight bets and one of them was a seven-leg parlay. "OK, what do you want me to do with these?"

"I fucked around and hit a seven-leg parlay from March Madness!" Brandon said.

"Yeah, OK! Let me check."

I scrolled through my phone and pulled up the scoreboard. One of the bets was a ticket for $50,000 on NC State, who won their game but did not cover the point spread of -6.5 against Oakland. That fifty grand would have paid $95,454. Another one was a two-team parlay on UConn and Marquette for $25,000. That 25 grand would have paid $90,000. The UConn team won and covered; Marquette won but didn't cover at -4.5 against Colorado. And there it was. The last ticket which was a $25,000 seven-team parlay with the odds of +9000. In betting layman's terms, the ticket pays 90 to 1. The parlay consisted of UConn -13.5, Purdue -11.5, Tennessee -6.5, Gonzaga -4, Arizona -8.5, UNC -4, and San Diego -5.5. Every one of the teams won and covered. This fool placed one of the chalkiest parlay bets in the history of sports gambling, and his lucky ass hit. The ticket was worth $2,250,000. "You're a multi-millionaire now, B!"

"I know. This was my ace in a hole plan."

A part of me knew that I could hang up on him, change my number, cash the ticket out, and go on with my life. The many business opportunities I could create with that amount of cash would set me up for life. But I am not that kind of friend. This was his win. Even if I knew he was unfit to manage that type of money, it was only fair that I do what was natural for me. "Yo! If you don't split that dough with me, I'm snitching!"

Brandon did not respond as several minutes passed by without him saying a word. One would hope that Brandon had died and I would be the sole proprietor of this ticket. But unfortunately, I heard him breathing hard as if he had been running. "Are you good?"

"Not really. Do me a favor. Take that winning ticket to the window, get the money, and bring it to me ASAP. I'll pay you handsomely for your time. I'm currently in San Diego. I'll text you my location," a winded Brandon said.

"Dope! I'll text you when I'm on my way."

"I'll need one more favor."

"Sure, what's up?"

"I want Justice's fucking watch! Help me bankrupt him. Oh, shit! I gotta go!" Brandon ended the call abruptly.

It sounded as if Brandon was being chased down. Holding on to this ticket generated mean thoughts because whatever did not kill Brandon at this juncture in life would disappoint me.

A lady who resembled the pictures from the dating app approached me, "Hey, are you Terrence?"

I stood to greet her. The lady was a lot more gorgeous in person. "You're LesFit?"

She laughed and extended her hand. "I'm Leslie. Leslie Thurman."

I sat across from the woman who had caught my attention the instant she walked into the cafe. Leslie had mischievously sparkling eyes and a smile that brightened the room.

"I'm sorry, I have to end our date so fast," I said. "But something came up and I need to get to San Diego ASAP."

"I love San Diego. It's by far my most favorite town in California," Leslie said.

I had a little time and money to play with. Besides, you miss 100 percent of all shots. So, I took one. "I know we just met, but would you be down to join me? I could use the company, and it would give us time to get to know each other."

A surprised smile yanked at the edges of Leslie's lips, and her eyes widened. "That sounds amazing. I'd be delighted."

"Dope! Let's pack a bag, hit the road, and see where this journey takes us."

Leslie's eyes twinkled with hope. "I can't wait to see what San Diego has in store for us."

I received a message from Brandon. It was his location. I clicked the link, and the GPS said I was 5 hours and 12 minutes away from him. I could not get rid of the sensation that I had just taken the first step toward something genuinely remarkable in my life. The possibilities were unlimited, and I was eager to find out where this road would lead.

THE END

ABOUT THE AUTHOR

Torthell Robinson was born on the Eaker Air Force Base located in Blytheville, Arkansas. He enlisted into the United States Air Force at age 17 and served as a Security Forces troop United States Air Force. During his military service, Torthell served two deployments to LSA Anaconda in Balad, Iraq (Operation Iraqi Freedom) and deployed to Manos, Kyrgyzstan (Operation Enduring Freedom). After separation from the military and with the help of the GI Bill, Torthell packed up and relocated to Los Angeles. There he advanced his knowledge in film production. Torthell studied at the Los Angeles Film School, the New York Film Academy, and UCB Upright Citizens Brigade, where he crafted his skill as a well-rounded writer.

Website: www.bookcollectionbyTorthell.com

Instagram: @Torthell

Twitter: @Torthell

Made in the USA
Middletown, DE
01 February 2025